WITHDRAWN

the JOURNEY to DRAGON ISLAND

CLAIRE FAYERS

HENRY HOLT AND COMPANY

NEW YORK

Henry Holt and Company
Publishers since 1866
175 Fifth Avenue
New York, New York 10010
mackids.com

Henry Holt® is a registered trademark of Macmillan Publishing Group, LLC.
Text copyright © 2017 by Claire Fayers
Chapter opener art copyright © 2017 by Oriol Vidal
All rights reserved.

Library of Congress Cataloging-in-Publication Data is available.
ISBN 978-1-62779-421-3

Our books may be purchased in bulk for promotional, educational, or business use.
Please contact your local bookseller or the Macmillan Corporate and
Premium Sales Department at (800) 221-7945 ext. 5442 or by e-mail at
MacmillanSpecialMarkets@macmillan.com.

First edition—2017 / Designed by Anna Booth

Printed in the United States of America by LSC Communications,
Harrisonburg, Virginia

1   3   5   7   9   10   8   6   4   2

To Gemma, for making this possible

PROLOGUE

LAWS OF ENERGY NUMBER ONE:
Energy cannot be created or destroyed; it can only be changed
from one form to another.
LAWS OF ENERGY NUMBER TWO:
Whenever energy is changed, the world will grow more chaotic.
(from ALDEBRAN BOSWELL'S BOOK OF SCIENTIFIC KNOWLEDGE)

Orion's Keep hung in the sky, as still as the stars overhead. The guardgoyles on the corner turrets leaned out, their spellstone eyes searching for intruders, but, as always, there were none. Even the teradons, which nested far below on Marfak's Peak, had learned to avoid it, and when a giant, flying dinosaur is afraid of a place, it's a good idea to stay far, far away.

But then, as the wind gusted and amber smoke billowed around the castle turrets, a shadow, almost the same black as the night sky, rose unsteadily. The guardgoyles were all staring straight out and had missed it completely. Even when the shadow hung directly below the castle, none of them reacted.

A metal spike arched upward with an almost-silent whoosh

and chinked into a gap between the stones. Then a rope unfurled and a figure began to climb.

Ten seconds later a guard on the castle walkway found out he was not alone. A thump and a muffled yelp, and a sword was snatched out of the air before it could make a sound.

The intruder stood cautiously, leaving the sword where it lay, and ran to the nearest tower. He'd made it: He was here and he was still alive. The impossible part was behind him, and the rest was going to be merely formidable.

He slipped inside the tower. As the door swung shut, it cut off the last pale glimmer of moonlight, and he almost shouted in panic. No wonder the magi were insane. Anyone would go mad, shut up inside these stones. He fumbled in his pocket for a lightstone and held it up. The glow barely penetrated the thick darkness, but gradually he was able to make out the walls on either side of him and a set of steps tumbling away into black invisibility. Keeping his free hand on the wall, he forced himself down them, his head swimming.

The steps opened into a passageway, dark except for one torch burning outside a barred door. The intruder's hands shook as he worked back the bolts.

Six beds stood in two rows, each one humped with the figure of a sleeping child. Two boys, two girls, two more boys. He ought to take them all with him, but there'd be no chance of getting out of here if he did. He'd come back, he promised silently.

He stopped by the last bed and bent close to the boy sleeping there. "Wake up," he murmured. "We're going home."

The boy opened his eyes. The intruder crouched so their faces were level, and smiled. "It's me."

The boy stared at him for a second. Then he opened his mouth and let out a scream that woke all the other children, and their cries brought guards running.

Y ou've broken Orion's Law," said the magus. "You know the penalty."

They were back on the castle battlements. The intruder stared defiantly at the guards and the three castle magi.

"You stole my son," he said. "Is it a crime to take him back?"

The magus limped forward, gripping his spellstaff with swollen fingers. "He belongs to the castle now. That was the agreement." Amber light snaked around his staff. "According to Orion's Law," he said, "you may choose where you die. What will it be? The Boiling Sands? The Lizard Swamp?"

The intruder tried not to stare at the light that crawled out of the spellstaff. He felt like he was standing on the edge of a deep, dark hole, plunging to almost-certain death.

And, oddly, he found that he didn't care. He dragged his gaze up to meet the magus's dark eyes. "Neither," he said. "I choose the sky."

He spun around, shoved the guards aside, and ran. One

of them shouted, but they were too late to stop him. All they could do was stand in shock as he vaulted over the castle battlements and disappeared into the night sky.

Everyone rushed to the edge and looked down. The sky was empty. There may have been a faint thump far below, but they'd probably imagined it. A body wouldn't hit the ground with enough force for it to be heard all the way up here. They waited awhile, just in case, but nothing moved and the night was cold, so they made their way back inside.

FOREWORD

Everyone knows the stories about the *Onion*. The most famous pirate ship on the eight oceans, captained by the unforgettable Cassie O'Pia and crewed by the fearsomest group of warriors ever to have left land. The *Onion* slew the Dreaded Great Sea Beast of the South, the *Onion* triumphed on the Island of Rats, the *Onion* stole all the treasure from the King of Camelopardalis and gave it to the people of Sadalbari.

More recently, however, the stories are all about how the *Onion* sailed to Magical North and came back full of magic just in time to defeat the evil magician Marfak West; saving the libraries of Barnard's Reach, where *all* stories have their home. And how, after they'd done all that, the crew sailed west in search of a long-forgotten island where dragons might live.

They must have fallen over the edge of the world by now because they haven't been seen since.

CHAPTER 1

Dragon eggs absorb magic. We know this—for centuries, magicians have collected the discarded shards, not knowing what they are. They call them starshell and use them for spellcasting. This uses up some of the magic in the world, but stories suggest that dragons themselves use much, much more. Yet dragons, with one exception, are extinct.

So, what happens to all the spare magic?

(from THOMAS GIRLING'S BOOK OF PIRATING ADVENTURES)

Brine Seaborne was bored. She shouldn't be—she was sunbathing on the deck of a pirate ship with a dragon in her lap. But after two months of sailing with a good wind, calm seas, and nobody attacking them, she was beginning to wish something would happen.

"Are you still keeping notes about our journey?" she asked Tom.

Tom looked up from his notebook. "Of course I am. Mum said it was important to keep accurate records so we can separate out the truth from the stories."

He'd grown taller in the past months, and the constant sunshine had tanned his skin an even brown. He still kept his dark brown hair long, and he wore his knee-length librarian's robe belted over his trousers. He said he needed it because of all the pockets, but Brine suspected he wore it because it reminded him of home in the underground libraries of Barnard's Reach.

"How much longer do you think it'll take us to find Dragon Island?" asked Brine. They'd passed the island of Auriga last week, which was the farthest west anyone had ever sailed before, so they must be getting close. Unless the people of Auriga were right, and if you carried on west, you'd sail off the edge of the world—which was nonsense, of course. Nowadays, everyone knew the world wasn't a bowl full of the sea, but a ball that had no edge or end.

"It'll take about an hour less than the last time you asked," said Peter, his shadow falling across her. The young magician sat down between Brine and Tom.

While Tom's skin had tanned in the sun, Peter's had developed pink patches, and his hair, which used to be dust-beige, had become the dirty yellow of dried sea-cabbage. He reached out to stroke Boswell's warm scales. The dragon let out a contented puff of flame and rolled over to let Peter scratch his belly where his scales were still pure silver. Over the past month, he'd been shedding, and the scales that grew back were the green of a stormy sea.

"Do you think we'll really find dragons on the Western Island?" asked Peter.

The rest of the crew didn't think so. Maybe there were dragons in the west once, but they were probably all extinct now—that was what pirate captain Cassie O'Pia and first mate Ewan Hughes said. And Tim Burre, who came from Auriga, was sure they'd fall off the edge of the world long before they found anything.

As far as most of the crew was concerned, they were sailing west in search of adventure and Brine's home—a home she still couldn't remember. Just because some of the books from Barnard's Reach talked about dragons, it didn't mean they'd find any. Brine knew that stories were usually made up out of a pinch of fact and several buckets of exaggeration, but even so, she couldn't help hoping.

"We *better* find dragons," said Tom. "My calculations show—"

"Yes, we know about your calculations." Peter grinned. "I'm telling you, the absence of dragons is not making the world fill up with magic. Excess magic burns off into the sky—it's how we get storms and the Stella Borealis. *Everyone* knows that."

"Then *everyone* is wrong," said Tom. "Some magic burns off, but not all of it. Dragons were supposedly the biggest consumer of magic in all of the eight oceans, but dragons have been extinct for so long that most people think they're just stories. Also, we've just lost Marfak West, and he used a lot of magic. So we've got a whole load of magical energy just hanging about the world, and increased magic means increased strangeness."

Brine started as Boswell gave a fiery snort, singeing her trousers. "I haven't noticed anything strange," she said, rubbing at the burnt fabric.

"Anyway, magic corrodes," said Peter. "That's why dragons build their nests out of gold and jewels, because they're the only things that don't disintegrate. Too much magic would make things fall apart. I'm a magician—I should know."

"You're a magician with a splinter of starshell in your hand," said Tom, raising his eyebrows. "But your hand hasn't fallen off yet."

"That's because the splinter is too small to make any difference." Peter sighed.

"What about this ship, then?" said Tom, patting the scuffed wooden deck of the *Onion*. "It's full of magic, and it hasn't fallen apart. And these"—he took his glasses off—"they belonged to Boswell the explorer, so how come they're exactly right for me?"

"Coincidence?" suggested Brine.

"Or maybe, the huge levels of magical energy concentrated at Magical North reshaped them to be what I needed," Tom argued. "Magic *changes* the world."

"Well, magic or not, right now I'd like the world to change to be a little more exciting," said Brine, shading her eyes as she peered at the featureless ocean. "In a good way, please—not with evil magicians trying to kill us."

Neither Tom nor Peter answered. Good—she'd finally gotten them off the subject of magic. Then she noticed how still they'd become.

"Umm . . . ," said Peter.

Something skittered on the deck behind them.

And then Cassie O'Pia shouted, "Giant spiders! Why is my ship full of giant spiders?"

Boswell fell off Brine's lap. Brine sat up in a hurry and put her hand back, straight through something that was warm and squished horribly. She shrieked.

"Don't just sit there screaming!" shouted Cassie. "All hands on spiders!"

Brine jumped up, shaking congealed spider off her hand. The rest of the gray-green spider lay behind her, a handprint through its crumpled body.

"That's gross," said Peter, his face matching the green of Boswell's scales.

"I know it's gross." Brine scrubbed her hand on her trousers. "Do something!"

Everywhere, pirates scrambled for weapons. More spiders came crawling over the deck rail. Brine counted at least twenty in a single glance. They were exactly the worst size imaginable. Big enough that you could count their eyes and see the slime hanging from their jaws. But small enough that they could scuttle straight up your body and cling to your face. Brine jumped back as a spider dropped from the rigging in front of Boswell. The little dragon toasted it with an enthusiastic belch of flame.

"They look like sea-spiders," said Tom with fascination, "though I've never seen a sea-spider that big before. Peter, did you magic them?"

"Of course I didn't!" Peter put a hand over his mouth. His eyes bulged as if he was going to be sick. "Why would I make giant spiders? I haven't done any magic since . . ."

Since Marfak West had captured him and made him do all sorts of terrible things, Brine thought. She shuddered.

Cassie rushed past, her long hair flying and her emerald pendant flashing against her bronze skin. Ewan Hughes was right behind her, as usual. Meanwhile, Trudi, the ship's cook, was trying to squash spiders with a frying pan.

"Remind me to scrub that before she uses it for cooking again," muttered Peter.

Never mind scrubbing it, Brine thought: She was going to throw it overboard.

An arrow hit the deck at her feet and she looked up to see Tim Burre in the crow's nest, waving a bow.

"Sorry!" he called cheerfully.

"They're only sea-spiders," Tom called back. "They're not dangerous!" He lifted his feet out of the way of one of them. "Just a million times bigger than they should be," he added uncertainly.

Cassie hacked down a sheet of green web from the mast.

"Tom, you're supposed to be killing them, not studying them. Squash them with a book or something."

Brine winced at the thought of Tom using a book as a weapon. She drew her sword and thrust it through a spider. The creature made a noise like wet leaves squishing underfoot, waved six of its eight legs at her, and died.

"Yuck," said Tom.

Boswell bounded across the deck on the heels of another spider. Did spiders have heels? Brine wondered. The dragon let off a burst of flame that missed the spider and set fire to a bucket.

"Nice job, Boswell," said Peter, running to grab him.

There were hardly any spiders left now, anyway. And then, after a few more minutes, there was only one, running in terrified circles. Cassie cut it in half and then threw the pieces into the sea.

"Well," she said, wiping slime off her cutlass, "that could have been worse."

Ewan Hughes clapped a hand on Peter's shoulder. "Peter, no one's blaming you for anything, but those creatures didn't look quite natural. Are you sure—"

"Yes, I'm sure," snapped Peter, adjusting his grip on Boswell and shrugging Ewan's hand aside. "Why does everyone keep blaming me?"

Because everyone was waiting for him to do something magical again, Brine thought. Magic was part of him. Peter giving up magic would be like Tom giving up books, or Cassie giving up the *Onion*. It simply couldn't be done. And it really didn't help that the pirates kept going on about magic when they knew Peter could be a bit touchy about the subject.

"He said he didn't do it," Brine said angrily as she kicked some dismembered spider legs into the ocean. "Leave him alone."

Peter turned on her. "I'm not a baby, and I don't need you looking after me." He dumped Boswell into her arms and stamped away to the ladder that led belowdecks.

Brine watched him go, a ball of hurt forming inside her. Peter wasn't just touchy, he was downright thorny, she thought. Like a hedgehog wrapped up in spinewood—with extra brambles.

Cassie rubbed at a dark patch of spider on her shirt. "He didn't mean it."

Deep down—very, very deep down—Brine knew that Cassie was right.

She set Boswell back on the deck, trying to look as if she weren't worried. In a way, it had been easier, when she and Peter had hated each other. She'd known the rules then— they made each other's lives as miserable as possible and they blamed each other for everything that went wrong. Now they were friends and she wanted to help him, but she didn't know how.

Ewan folded his arms. "So if Peter didn't do this, who did?"

"Maybe the sea-spiders are bigger out west," said Bill Lightning. He grinned and sheathed his sword. "I'm glad they were *small* giant spiders. Last time we fought spiders, they were as big as camels and had eighteen legs each. Terrifying."

"But we're pirates," added Rob Grosse. "We laugh in the face of terror."

The crew immediately started comparing stories of all the giant spiders they'd fought. Brine stayed silent. She didn't believe Bill had fought spiders of any size before. She wanted to go after Peter, but she was afraid it would only make things worse. She picked up a broom from the side of the deck and started sweeping spider legs into the sea.

Tom came to help her. "Good idea. Let's get rid of them before Trudi starts wondering how to make eight-legged casserole," he whispered. Then he paused, frowning at the hairy remains scattered across the deck. "Sea-spiders eat wood, right? A hundred times their own weight in an hour."

Bill Lighting paused halfway through a story about how he'd defeated a swarm of giant scorpions single-handedly. "Right. They lay their eggs on rafts made of spiderweb, then the web attaches to the next ship that comes along, and the eggs hatch. The spiders eat for a while then spin another raft and lay more eggs. They're a nuisance, but generally nothing to worry about. Giant scorpions, on the other hand . . ."

"But what if the sea-spiders weren't eating just any old wood?" interrupted Tom. "Think about it. The old *Onion* was an ordinary pirate ship. . . ."

"There was nothing ordinary about her," growled Cassie.

Tom flushed pink. "I know. I mean she was *made* of

ordinary wood. But the new *Onion* was moored at Magical North for a hundred years. It changed her into something magical, and just because she's settled down into a pirate ship now—it doesn't mean the magic has gone. Her wood is full of it. What do you think would happen to a spider if it ate a hundred times its own weight in magic?"

Cassie twisted the emerald around her neck. "I suppose the spider might grow," she admitted. She walked to the side of the deck and stared down at the sea, as if wondering what else might emerge.

"Is this what you meant?" Brine asked Tom. "When you said that without dragons, there's too much magic in the world—and increased magic means increased strangeness?" She hadn't really believed him before, but if this was what magic did to something as tiny as a sea-spider, maybe Tom was right after all.

Tom tucked his hair behind his ears and nodded. "The books I've read say dragons consume magic, so as there haven't been any sightings of dragons for hundreds of years, well . . . apart from Boswell"—he gestured at the dragon who was locked in a tug-of-war over a spider leg with the ship's cat, Zen—"then the amount of excess magic must have been going up all this time. We could be reaching an unsustainable level."

Ewan Hughes frowned. "We're pirates, not scientists. Can you use smaller words?"

"He means giant spiders are the least of our worries," said

Brine. "Unless we do something to reduce the level of magic in the world, this sort of thing is just going to happen more often."

"More spiders," said Tom. "And strange weather, and magical creatures . . . Remember the fish-birds and snow bears from Magical North? Things like that, popping up all over the eight oceans."

"Right," said Cassie uncertainly. "So either we find a load more magicians and get them casting spells, or we find more dragons."

"Dragons," said Ewan Hughes. "Let's find dragons. I hate magicians." He caught Brine's glare. "All magicians except Peter, I mean."

CHAPTER 2

SEA-SPIDER CURRY

Take several giant sea-spiders—as many as you can fit in a frying pan. Fry gently with lots of onions and a whole tub of curry powder until you start to choke on the smoke, then fill the pan up with water. Simmer for an hour then serve or throw away.

(from COOKING UP A STORME— THE RECIPES OF A GOURMET PIRATE)

Everybody was so used to Peter needing time on his own that when he climbed down the ladder to the lower level of the ship, nobody commented. That was the best thing about being a magician, he thought. You could do what you liked, and everyone assumed you were busy with secret magicky things.

Of course, being a magician had its disadvantages. Such as everyone's assumption that if something strange happened, it had to be your fault. And the way the crew kept trying extra hard to be nice to him. As if they thought Peter was on the edge of a mental breakdown and had to be handled as carefully as starshell—in case he cracked and turned them all into worms, like he'd done to the Mother Keeper of Barnard's Reach. The crew didn't know Peter still had nightmares about it. He kept telling himself it hadn't been his fault, but it didn't make any difference. Because of him, the Mother Keeper was living in a jar, eating leaves, and Tom's mother was in charge of Barnard's Reach.

Peter paused at the bottom of the steps in case Brine was planning on following him. Thank goodness she was as irritating as ever. Peter needed that because it felt normal, and right now he didn't think anything else was ever going to be normal again.

He still wasn't quite used to the feel of the new *Onion*. The old *Onion* had two levels belowdecks, but this ship only had one. Cassie had taken the captain's cabin at the prow end. Then there was Trudi's galley, a small workroom, and the sleeping quarters where the pirates took it in turns to occupy the hammocks because there weren't quite enough of them. And, finally, right at the back, a storage area where wooden crates were stacked up right to the ceiling.

Zen, the ship's cat, slunk past Peter's ankles, a well-chewed spider's leg dangling mustache-like from his mouth. Tom's messenger seagull opened its eyes, decided that Peter was boring, and then went back to sleep. Peter picked up a lantern and made his way past the hammocks and discarded piles of stripy socks and underpants to the back of the ship. He'd found out that if you squeezed between the third and fourth storage crate—you had to be small to do it—you'd end up in a narrow gap where no one could see you.

It was the closest thing to privacy Peter had been able to find on the ship. He squeezed through, then set the lantern on the floor and sat down next to the light, his back pressed against one crate and his knees squashed up against another. The crew meant well—it wasn't their fault they kept eyeing him like he was a poisonous blowfish about to explode. They were doing their best, but they were afraid of magic, especially after what had happened with Marfak West.

And yet, if you gathered all their fears together and multiplied them by a million, they still wouldn't come close to the heart-stopping terror Peter felt every time he thought about casting a spell.

Peter drew in a shaky breath and wiped his hands over his face. He'd gone through this a thousand times. He needed to discover himself again, he thought. He'd been a magician for so long that he couldn't remember what he was like before— Peter without the magic. He just hoped the crew would give him the time to work it out. Brine, too. Peter had given all his starshell pieces to her, and it had seemed right at the time. But their adventure to Magical North had changed Brine. She was the *Onion*'s Chief Planning Officer now, and she thought she had to have a plan to fix absolutely everything. She didn't seem to realize there were some things that just couldn't be fixed.

Peter nudged the lantern, making the shadows jump. One

of them stretched up taller than the rest, and if you stared at it for too long, it began to look like a person. A man, to be precise, tall and bald and wearing a cloak. Peter couldn't take his eyes off it. Marfak West the magician was dead. Peter knew he was dead because he'd been there when it had happened. He'd watched Boswell's egg explode in the magician's hands and blow him to pieces.

Most of all, Peter knew Marfak West was dead because otherwise his ghost couldn't be grinning down at him right now.

"Well," said the dead man, "this is very cozy."

Marfak West looked much the same as he had in life except a little more see-through. A rim of shadow surrounded him, as black as the flecks in his amber eyes.

Peter sat still and said nothing, feeling his heart beating ever so slightly faster.

The first time Marfak West had appeared, Peter had assumed, quite reasonably, that he'd gone insane. After being almost drowned twice, swallowed alive by a whale, and forced to help Marfak West in his attempt to destroy Barnard's Reach, it was no wonder Peter was seeing things.

"Dragon got your tongue?" asked Marfak West.

Peter brought his thoughts back under control. Marfak West couldn't hurt him now. "You're not real," he said shakily. "I don't know why you keep hanging around."

"Because it's more entertaining than the afterlife," said the ghost of Marfak West. "I don't know what you're fussing about. It's not like I've tried to tempt you to sink the ship or kill Cassie."

"Yet . . ." said Peter. And he tried not to think about how much he'd missed this. Even though Marfak West was pure evil. Even though he had used Peter, played on his fears, and taught him magic only so he could betray him later. He'd tortured him and threatened to kill him. And yet his absence had left a gap. When he was with Marfak West, Peter had been able to exercise some part of himself that no one else understood.

Peter stood up. "You're not going to trick me again. If you don't leave me alone, I'm going to tell Cassie about you."

"Go ahead and tell her," said the ghost. "Tell her you've been having conversations with the man you murdered. Cassie will know what to do. Do they have somewhere safe to lock you up on this ship?" He grinned. "I bet they could build something out of the packing crates for you, and you can go mad all by yourself in the dark."

"I'm not going mad," said Peter, hating the uncertainty in his own voice. Mad or not, he knew that Marfak West was right. If Peter told Cassie about this, she wouldn't care whether he was haunted or hallucinating—she'd make sure someone was watching him every single second. He'd never have a moment to himself. For Cassie, the *Onion* always came first.

"You shouldn't blame Cassie," said Marfak West, almost sympathetically. "Whatever the stories say about her, she's just an ordinary sailor, and you are a most extraordinary magician. You must be—you killed me, after all."

Peter punched a crate and immediately regretted it. "Will you stop saying that?" he hissed, rubbing his smarting knuckles. "I didn't kill you—you grabbed the dragon's egg and it blew up. It was your own fault."

"Then you have nothing to worry about," said Marfak West. "You can go back to using magic because you've only ever used it for safe, happy things, never to hurt or kill."

Peter looked away from him. Of course he wanted to use magic again. He wanted the feeling of power in his hands, the satisfaction of drawing a perfect spellshape into the air and releasing the spell to do its work. Even more than that, he yearned for the freedom he'd felt when he'd found out that he didn't need spellshapes, that true magic was all about experimentation and rule-breaking and going as far as his imagination could take him. In other words, to some very dark places indeed.

Peter sighed.

"What's happened to make you miserable this time?" asked the ghost.

"Nothing's happened. That's the problem." The spiders had been the first thing that had happened in weeks, and it had almost been a relief to have something to do. Brine was bored, Tom was bored, even Cassie was becoming restless, and when Cassie got bored, it was time to get worried.

"Do dragons consume magic?" he asked. "Tom thinks the amount of magic in the world has been increasing and that's why strange things are happening."

"You're a magician. More magic is a good thing." Marfak West casually leaned back against the crates. Could ghosts lean? Peter wondered. Shouldn't Marfak West go straight through? He sighed. He definitely had too much time on his hands when he started wondering how the laws of physics governed his delusions.

"You might be interested to know," said Marfak West, still leaning, "that while you lot have been messing about up on deck, I've had a nice chat with the *Onion*."

Great. Now his delusion was developing delusions. "You do know that ships can't talk, right?" said Peter.

"Yes, they can, especially when they're this full of magic. It's just that nobody ever takes the time to listen. Given that I've got a lot of time and not much to do with it, I've been listening."

Peter tried to look as if he didn't care. "What's the *Onion* been saying, then?"

"Nothing much. Only that you won't need to worry about boredom for much longer. You know what they say, don't you? Sail west past Auriga, and first the sea will stop moving and then you'll fall off the edge of the world."

That old story again. Peter picked up the lantern. "We're not going to fall off the edge of the world. The world is a ball—there's no edge." Without waiting for an answer, he squeezed out through the crates. A ripple of laughter followed him as he hurried back to the steps.

He stopped at the bottom, looking up at the patch of sky through the hatch. He didn't want to stay here with Marfak West, but he couldn't face another round of worried looks from the crew, either.

Something bumped into his knees, then burped fire over his shoes.

"Boswell," said Peter.

The little dragon nudged at his knees again. Not worried, not wanting him to be something he wasn't, just wanting some company. Peter sat down against the bottom rung of the ladder and let Boswell clamber onto his lap. "If you eat magic," he said, "why aren't you eating the ship?"

Boswell snorted, sounding so outraged that Peter laughed. He stroked the dragon's head. The dark spot on his palm where the starshell chip was lodged felt cool. He hadn't cast a spell for so long, the starshell should be buzzing with magic, but he could barely tell it was there. Maybe Boswell really was consuming the excess.

Boswell tried to climb inside Peter's shirt. When he was newly hatched, he used to fit—Peter still had the claw and singe marks to prove it. Now, the dragon could only get his head and shoulders inside. Not for the first time, Peter wondered what would happen to Boswell when he outgrew the ship.

Peter detached the dragon's claws from his front. "Don't

worry," he said, sure that Boswell wasn't worried at all. "We'll find Dragon Island for you."

The light from the hatch dimmed. "Peter?" said Brine. "The crew is busy if you want to come out."

Peter looked up. "I know the crew's busy. I'm sitting here with Boswell."

Brine appeared slightly disappointed that he wasn't in the middle of a breakdown. Peter wondered whether he ought to tell her about Marfak West, but the ghost was already fading from his mind. Maybe later, Peter thought, once they were safely past the edge of the world and Marfak West was proved wrong. He moved Boswell aside and climbed back up the ladder.

"I was thinking," said Brine, "if Tom's right, the starshell in your hand will be overflowing with magic. You ought to cast a spell. Just a simple one to get rid of the excess."

Sometimes Peter wished there was a spell that could make Brine leave him alone. But he doubted even magic could achieve that. "Honestly," he said, "I'm fine. Don't worry." He looked around for Tom and spotted him scraping spiderweb off the mast and examining it. "Tom, can I borrow one of your books about dragons and magic?"

Tom wiped his fingers on his library robe. "Yes, of course. As long as you promise to take care of it and return it by the due date."

"The due date? We're on the same ship. What do you think I'm going to do—jump overboard with it?"

Tom grinned. "Oh, right. I guess we don't really need the library rules here. I'll get the whole box for you and you can read whichever ones you like."

"Since when did you want to read?" Brine asked Peter as Tom scurried off, librarian-like.

Peter gave her a grin. "Since I thought books might be interesting."

Books were actually a good way to hide in plain view, Peter found. He could sit on the deck in the sun, and, apart from Trudi coming over once to ask if he was reading anything good, everyone left him alone. He didn't even notice how quiet it had grown until he happened to glance up and he saw that the ship was barely moving.

Cassie was standing at the prow of the ship, gazing into the distance. "I don't like the look of this sea," she said as Brine and Peter approached.

The sea looked fine to Peter. It was flat and calm and not doing much, but it wasn't trying to drown, freeze, or eat them. "It could be worse," he said, expecting Cassie to agree with him. Instead, she frowned.

"Worse is in the eye of the beholder. When the weather is bad, we can fight it. But no weather at all? That's a different matter. Without wind, we're stuck."

As if to prove her point, the last shred of breeze died, and the *Onion* glided to a standstill.

Tim Burre gave a moan. "I told you. It's the great stillness before the end of the world. We're all going to die."

CHAPTER 3

Another ship has disappeared in the rectangle of sea between the islands of Acamar and Betria in the Agena Ocean.
This so-called Agena Rectangle has now claimed eight ships,
all vanished without a trace. Baron Mora of Acamar blames
all the magicians who have moved to the island, recently
claiming that starshell recharges faster there.

(from STRANGE TIDES: JOURNAL OF THE UNEXPLAINED AND
INEXPLICABLE, Submitted to Barnard's Reach by news-scribe)

Despite Tim Burre's prediction of doom, the wind was the
only thing that died. The *Onion* bobbed gently on a flat
sea, barely making any progress. With nothing else to do,
Brine raided the galley for leftover meat and took Boswell up
on the main deck for a flying lesson. "Come on," she said,
holding a piece of meat up high. "Come and get it."

Boswell tried to lick his own backside, overbalanced, and
landed on his nose. Then he sat and stared at Brine mourn-
fully until guilt got the better of her and she gave him the
meat anyway.

Bill Lightning stopped to watch. "You should take him up to the top of the mast and drop him if you want him to fly. It's how my dad taught me to swim."

"Your father threw you from the top of a mast?" said Brine.

Bill grinned and nodded. "Luckily we only had a small boat, so it wasn't too high. Even luckier still that I landed in the sea and not on the deck, or I'd have gone straight through. Boswell's a dragon. He's got to learn to toughen up."

"He's the last of his kind, for all we know," Peter said, looking up from Tom's books. "If anything happens to him, we'll have lost the only dragon in the world."

"We'll find more. Don't worry." Bill slapped her on the shoulder. "He's probably just a bit young. Try it again in a month if we're still alive. He'll learn when he needs to."

Tim Burre stamped past them. "I told you. It's the Great Stillness. Either we'll all die of thirst here, or we'll start moving again and fall off the edge of the world."

He sounded pleased to be proved right. If the ship fell off the edge of the world, he probably wouldn't even notice, Brine thought, he'd be so busy shouting, *I told you so!*

"If the world ends just after Auriga," she said, "how can I come from an island farther west?"

Tim Burre's forehead crinkled. "Magic." He leaned closer. "I know a ship that sailed west—it came back in pieces. Crushed against the edge of the world."

So the edge of the world was a wall now, not a rim you

could fall off. "You can't really believe that," said Brine. "Why did you stay on the ship if you thought we were all doomed?"

Tim Burre glanced across to where Cassie was standing at the helm. "Because if there's one person who can survive falling off the world," he said, "it's Cassie O'Pia. I reckoned it was worth a try." He squinted into the distance. "Are those mountains?"

Brine's heart gave a jump as she saw them, too—a cluster of peaks, shimmering in the distance, rising straight out of the sea. "Told you," she said. "There's no such thing as the end of the world." She tossed Boswell the rest of the meat. "Cassie!"

"I see them. Full speed to starboard."

The *Onion* drifted around gently, ambled across a ripple or two, and paused.

"All right, so full speed might be a little slower than usual," said Cassie as everyone groaned.

►⋯⊹⊹⊹ӏ●

The hours passed and the *Onion* crept across the motionless sea, but the mountains appeared as far away as ever. Cassie gave orders with her usual confidence, but Brine saw the frown lines around her eyes. The crew was used to fighting their way out of dangerous situations. If a giant squid rose from the deep now and attacked them, they'd go for it with cheers of joy. But they couldn't fight this . . . this nothing.

As evening drew on, Brine sat with Peter and Tom and watched. Without the usual noise of wind in the sails, the pulsing of wood was unusually loud: a steady, rhythmic beat that sounded almost like the ship was breathing. It was the sound of the magic filling the ship, Peter had said once, expanding and contracting. Brine had no idea how he knew that or how she could hear it, because only magicians were supposed to be able to sense magic.

"I don't like this," said Rob Grosse for about the twentieth time.

Brine shaded her eyes, squinting at the horizon. "Is it magic?" She turned her head slowly from side to side, watching the mountains. They seemed to blur on the edge of her vision, turning to mist, but as she looked straight at them, they became solid again.

Tom shook his head. "Actually, I think it's entirely natural. What we're seeing is a mirage. It's very rare, but when the sky and sea are both really clear, sailors sometimes see islands that aren't there."

"And you've read about this in your books, have you?" asked Ewan.

Tom gave him a puzzled look. "I've read about everything in my books."

Cassie strode across the deck. "Whatever it is, we're not going to find out sitting here. Peter, I know you've given up magic for now, but can't you conjure up some wind for us?"

Brine felt Peter shift beside her. She kept her gaze on the sea, careful not to turn and meet his gaze.

"You can't just create wind," said Tom. "Wind is air that's

31

moving. Think of how much air you'd have to move just to get a breeze."

"It's air," grumbled Rob. "It's not like it's heavy."

The sun dipped below the horizon and, as the sky darkened, the mountains disappeared.

"There we are," said Tom. "Mirage."

Brine heard a flapping sound behind her. "Well done, Boswell," she said. He was finally getting the hang of what his wings were for.

But when she turned around, she saw the dragon curled up with Zen, asleep. She looked up—to the very top of the mainmast, where the black-and-white flag hung like a rag. The bottom edge of it waved at her.

Around the deck, the pirates paused. Nobody dared say anything in case this was another mirage. Tom opened his notebook and held it up. Some of the pages fluttered gently.

"Wind!" shouted Tim Burre. "Wind ahoy!"

A moment later a gust caught the sails, bowing them out. The pirates cheered as the *Onion* picked up speed. Brine stood, a huge grin on her face. "I knew Tim Burre was making things up about the end of the world."

They were on their way to the Western Island again, she thought. She'd find her family, and it would turn out that they were the last dragon trainers in the world. They'd adopt Boswell and prepare him for a life in the wild. Brine would be sad to see him go, of course, but he'd come back to the island every year to visit and she'd be known as the Dragon Girl of the West.

She turned to face Peter. "We will find dragons," she said.

She'd expected him to disagree, but he nodded. "I know," he said, frowning at her.

"What's wrong?" Brine asked.

"Nothing."

It didn't look like nothing was wrong. It looked like something was very wrong indeed, but that Peter didn't want to tell her. Brine crossed her arms. "If you don't say, I'll tell Cassie to throw you overboard."

Peter barely smiled at the joke. "All right, then. Marfak West's ghost is on board."

"That's not funny," said Tom, frowning.

Peter crossed his arms. "It's not supposed to be. Marfak West is on the ship and I've talked to him—down below-decks."

Brine scratched her head. Peter didn't look mad, and she knew he wasn't joking, because he wouldn't joke about Marfak West. "I've had nightmares about him, too," she said. "But he's gone. He can't hurt us now. The ship has all sorts of dark places belowdecks. And you get odd shadows. . . ."

"You think I can't tell the difference between a shadow and Marfak West?" Peter flushed with anger. "I'll show you—come on."

They followed Peter down the steps. Tom's messenger

gull squawked at them, making Brine jump. There was a perfectly good explanation for this, she reminded herself. Peter had suffered at the hands of Marfak West more than any of them. He'd probably thought he'd seen something in the dark.

"He said we were all going to die," said Peter. He pointed to the dark stacks of crates at the back of the ship. "Through there."

Brine looked at the dark gap between the crates. She couldn't see anything, but she caught her breath as Tom squeezed past her.

"I can't see anything."

He squirmed out and Brine took his place. She could hear her own breath unsteady in her ears. Marfak West was more likely to appear to her than to Tom. *If* his ghost were here, which it couldn't be because . . . well, why would it be? Ghosts haunted places like the Sea of Sighs; they didn't stand around admiring packing crates.

Something touched her face and she jumped, but it was only a strand of spider's web—normal-sized. She pushed her way back out quickly. "Nothing." She grinned with relief. "It must have been your imagination."

"But—" started Peter.

He was interrupted by alarm bells ringing overhead.

Brine promptly forgot about *probably* nonexistent ghosts and tore up the steps to the deck.

"The end of the world!" shouted Tim Burre. "The end of the world, ahoy!"

In the flood of silver moonlight, Brine saw a great line of water stretching out, and, beyond that, a broad lip of land narrowed to a point that looked like the spout of a jug. And all the waters of the ocean poured up and over it, in a great unending rush that made no sound at all as it tumbled into a great, black void, empty save for the shining lights of the stars.

"Man the sails!" yelled Cassie. "Turn this ship around!"

The crew shook themselves out of their daze and stumbled to obey. But the *Onion* continued relentlessly on course, heading straight for that tumbling line of water, beyond which there was no ocean—nothing at all.

CHAPTER 4

It's the end of the sea; we're all going to die.
We'll fly with Orion up into the sky.
The wreck of our ship will become a new star.
It's the end of the world, and it's not very far.

(from OVER THE EDGE by Tim Burre)

Peter couldn't get his brain and his eyes to agree on what he was seeing. The world didn't have an edge, his brain said. The world was round like a ball. It was one of those things he'd always known, just like he knew that fire burned and that his old master, Tallis Magus, would beat him around the ears anytime he got a spellshape wrong.

And that shows how much you know, said his eyes. Because, if the world was a ball, what was that rapidly approaching ridge of land? And the sea pouring over the side like water out of a bucket?

Behind him, Rob Grosse began to laugh hysterically. "It's the brim. We're going out of the bowl."

"Turn this ship around!" screamed Cassie. She slashed the

rope holding the mainsail, and the canvas sagged limply, but the ship didn't slow. The sea rushed on and they rushed on with it.

"My books!" cried Tom. He rushed across the deck to gather them up from where Peter had left them.

Brine gripped Peter's arm. "Peter . . ."

"I know. Do something." He couldn't do anything. He couldn't even move. The deck lurched beneath his feet. If he tried to take a step, he'd fall down: He knew it.

"Abandon ship!" Bill Lightning yelled, and in a moment everyone was shouting. Brine let go of Peter and ran.

Peter took a step after her and found to his surprise that he hadn't fallen down after all. The deck still felt like it was heaving, but when he stood still, everything seemed to grow quiet. The sound of the ocean pouring off the world should be deafening, and yet the only noise came from the crew as they fought over the rowing boats and tried to turn the *Onion* around.

Where was Tom? He'd know what was going on. Peter spotted him a moment later, his hands full of books, trying to stop Ewan Hughes from slashing the sails to pieces. Ewan didn't seem to care where he was waving his cutlass. Peter ran and caught his arm.

"Get out of the way," snapped Ewan.

Peter clenched his fingers over the dark spot on his right palm and drew a shape in the air with his left hand instead. "Back off or I'll turn you into a jellyfish."

The threat worked. Only for two seconds, but it was long

enough for Peter to drag Tom out of the way. Ewan went back to attacking the sails.

"They'll destroy the ship," said Tom. "We have to stop them." His eyes were wide behind his glasses.

Peter grabbed his arm. "Come on."

He looked around for Brine and saw her fighting Trudi over one of the rowing boats. Then Bill Lightning grabbed the boat, hurled it over the side of the ship, and prepared to jump after it, but twenty pirates piled on top of him. Brine tumbled backward, scrambled up, and started clambering over them all.

"Brine, stop!" Peter leaped for her and hauled her off the heap of squirming pirates. They both crashed to the deck. Brine kicked him in the face, and his vision flared amber for a second.

Tom sat on her legs. "Brine, it's a mirage. Listen!"

Brine kept trying to kick them. Boswell scampered across and burrowed into Peter, whimpering. Looking over the side of the ship, Peter saw the rowing boat bob away and suddenly disappear.

"A mirage?" Brine said, her face pressed into the deck. "Like the mountains?"

Peter nodded. The movement made his head feel like it was going to fall off. He sat back on his heels and rested his hand on Boswell's back. He could still see the edge of the world hurtling toward them, but they weren't getting any closer.

Brine pushed Tom off. "Why didn't you say so? Where's Cassie?"

The pirate captain staggered by right at that moment, grappling with Rob Grosse. Brine grabbed hold of her as she passed. "Stop fighting! This isn't real."

"Nobody tells me to stop fighting," snarled Cassie, shaking her off.

Peter hung on to Rob's sword arm. "We're not telling you. We're asking you . . . nicely . . . to stop. We're not going to fall over the edge of the world." He tried to think of something that would convince her. "It's magic," he said.

"Magic?" Cassie paused. Rob stopped struggling, too, now that Cassie wasn't trying to hit him.

Tom nodded. "Remember I said there was too much magic? It's making us see things."

Cassie sucked in a breath. "Are you sure?"

"Listen," said Tom. Cassie tilted her head to one side. After a moment she frowned and sheathed her cutlass.

"Stupid magic making us do stupid things," she muttered. She swung away from Rob and strode over to Ewan, who was still trying to cut down the sails. "Everyone, stop!" she shouted. She pulled Ewan away from the rigging. "This isn't real."

Turning, Peter saw that the foaming edge of the ocean was rushing closer. He staggered and clutched Brine for balance. It was only a mirage, he reminded himself.

Cassie stood still. "If you're wrong about this—we're all going to die in about thirty seconds."

Peter's face ached from the effort of not screaming. He gritted his teeth into a smile. "Don't worry. Magicians are never wrong."

The *Onion* climbed the last wave and plunged down. Peter had to bite his own hand to keep himself from screaming. Brine gripped his other hand, her nails digging in— she looked like she was holding her breath.

The ship shot out of the sea altogether and into the bank of land that formed the spout of the bowl. They hung for a second, teetering right on the edge, then slowly toppled over. Even though Peter knew it wasn't happening, his stomach lurched and he shut his eyes tight.

The moment he did, the deck leveled out beneath him, the rush of movement stilled, and he knew they'd never been falling at all. He kept his eyes closed and marveled that he could still feel the waves lifting the ship up and down, and hear the sea slapping against the hull.

"You're hurting my hand," he said finally.

"Sorry." Brine let go.

Peter opened his eyes. The ocean stretched out around them, flat and wide and endless, just like oceans ought to be. He'd never seen anything so amazing, so beautiful. He wanted to jump into the sea and kiss the waves.

The pirates cheered. Cassie clapped Peter on the back and laughed. "Well done. Everyone, get back to work. We've just survived the Great Stillness. The Western Island can't be far. Nothing else is going to go wrong."

Nothing, except for a patch of water that had started to heave as if it were boiling. Then something rose out of the sea straight ahead of them—something huge and with far, far too many tentacles.

Ewan Hughes drew his cutlass. "That'd better be another mirage."

CHAPTER 5

A severe monster warning is in place for all ships on the Atlas Ocean this month. Be on the lookout for giant crabs, flying sharks, and swarms of man-eating squid. We advise postponing all nonessential journeys.

(from the BARNARD'S REACH MONSTER FORECAST)

The monster was so big that Brine had to look at it in pieces. First, tentacles—giant brown ones sprouting out of the sea like a forest come suddenly to life, then slender green ones that waved in between. They couldn't possibly all be part of the same animal, Brine thought, but then the waters shifted and she glimpsed the huge moving mass where the tentacles met.

"It's the Dreaded Great Sea Beast of the South all over again," groaned Bill. Then he grinned and drew his sword. "This is more like it."

After months of easy sailing with very little to do, the pirates greeted the monster with the enthusiasm of long-lost friends. Brine backed off as they rushed to attack. A tentacle slapped down on the deck, scattering half the crew, but they were up on their feet again in an instant, and they fell upon the creature with yells and whoops.

Brine caught hold of Peter and Tom, and they all edged toward the back of the ship, away from the worst of the tentacles.

"Do you think we should help?" Tom asked, sounding like he'd rather not.

Brine shook her head. "I think they've got this covered."

Cassie chopped through her first tentacle and waved it over her head like a flag. The monster snatched it out of her hands, lifting her off her feet for a moment before she let go. Meanwhile, Bill Lightning, Ewan, and Rob Grosse were slashing at any bits of sea-monster that came close enough. Trudi waved a meat cleaver in wild circles.

Brine felt oddly sorry for the beast. It must have thought it had found an easy meal but was realizing its mistake now.

"Go for the eyes!" cried Cassie.

"Aye, aye!" Ewan shouted back, and the air filled with arrows.

Boswell rushed at the tentacles, growling and flapping his wings, and Brine's heart leaped into her mouth. "Boswell, come back here!" She lunged for him and missed. A tentacle hit the mainmast, and the *Onion* tilted sideways. Brine staggered and slid.

"Hold on!" yelled Cassie as more tentacles wrapped around the mast and pulled. The *Onion* rose half out of the sea. Peter grabbed Brine's hand, which only meant the two of them slid down the deck together.

The *Onion* tilted farther, spilling screaming pirates into the sea. Ewan Hughes clawed his way up the deck and started smacking at the tentacles with both daggers, but the monster clung on tighter, pulling the *Onion* over and down into the sea. Brine's feet hit the deck rail. She was practically standing on it, her back against the deck and Peter clinging to her hand. She looked down and immediately wished she hadn't. The dark waves churned hungrily and several pirates thrashed about, trying to stay afloat. Oddly, the monster paid them no attention, though it could have picked them out of the sea.

Tom landed in a heap beside them with Boswell on top of him. Zen's claws scraped across the deck as the cat slid down to join them and thumped into Tom's head.

"Funny," said Tom, spitting out fur, "the monster seems more interested in the ship than in us."

Brine tried to hang on to the deck. "Oh good. Then it might let us drown instead of eating us."

Boswell untangled himself from Tom and started clawing determinedly up the deck. Brine grabbed for him and missed. "Boswell, come here!"

Peter let go of Brine's hand and tried to climb up the deck after the dragon.

Boswell sprang at a tentacle. Brine expected to see the dragon swatted aside, and she opened her mouth to shout.

But the tentacle stopped moving and, as Boswell took a bite out of the end, it began to shrink.

"What?" said Brine in disbelief.

All over the ship, tentacles slowly unfurled, including the one wrapped around the mainmast. The *Onion* slapped back into the water with a jolt that knocked Brine flat. Boswell trotted over to her and spat a long string of seaweed onto her head.

"It's a plant," said Tom, picking the slimy green mass out of her hair. "I don't believe it. The whole thing is one gigantic plant."

Brine scrambled up onto her knees, staring as a giant body rose out of the water, easily as big as the *Onion*. Boswell attacked another tentacle, then another. The waving arms looked far more like branches now, and the body was full of lumps and dips. Not just one plant, but loads of them all squashed together.

Boswell flapped up onto the now-horizontal deck rail and blew out a stream of flame, then he lifted his head and made a noise that Brine had never heard before.

Peter staggered to his feet. "He's trying to roar."

It sounded more like the noise Zen might make after eating Trudi's spider-leg curry, but Peter was right, Brine thought. She ran to Boswell and wrapped her arms around the dragon's warm scaly neck. "Well done."

"All those in favor of letting the monster eat the ship, say aye!" shouted Cassie. A few plantlike tentacles swept back at her and she chopped them away. But the monster was shrinking back, retreating into the water. Within a minute all that was left was a patch of churning white waves where it had disappeared.

Ewan dropped ropes to the crew who were still thrashing around in the water. Brine watched them climb, shivering, back on board. It was no wonder ships that sailed west from Auriga came back in pieces, Brine thought. First the Great Stillness, then the end of the world, and anyone who hadn't abandoned ship by then would find themselves tangled up in vegetable tentacles.

"Why did it stop attacking?" asked Trudi. She sounded disappointed, as if she'd forgotten how close they'd all come to drowning. Brine hadn't forgotten, and she kept a tight hold of the deck rail, just in case the plant monster reappeared.

"Did you see how the tentacle turned to seaweed when Boswell grabbed it?" asked Tom. "I think he might have taken all the magic out of it."

Peter flexed his fingers. "And . . . I think he might have been doing it all along but none of us noticed. The starshell piece in my hand hasn't given me any trouble for ages."

"You're constantly touching Boswell," said Brine. That made sense—as much as anything else did today.

Tom began collecting bits of seaweed from the deck. "I'll add it to my list of things we don't know. It's a shame we didn't get the chance to study the plant monster more closely."

Brine felt she'd studied it as much as she wanted to. She turned full circle, enjoying the lack of mirages or monsters. In every direction she saw the same thing: the calm, dark waters of the Western Ocean, rising and falling.

Actually, that wasn't quite true. Right ahead of them, where there was still a faint glow of golden light on the horizon, a black lump rose out of the sea. It was too big to be a ship and too still to be another monster. It could be a mirage, but the last mirage had disappeared as night had fallen.

Brine's breath caught in her throat.

"Land ahoy!" shouted Tim Burre, quite unnecessarily.

The Western Island—Dragon Island. At last, Brine was within sight of home. She stared at the shape in the ocean, looking for something, *anything* she recognized. She was so sure she'd remember the place when she saw it, but none of it looked familiar.

"You should sleep," said Cassie. "We'll be there by morning."

Brine nodded and stumbled away, glad to get away on her own for once. Tomorrow, when she awoke, she'd be home. They'd go ashore and explore and she'd find her parents and a whole colony of dragons, and she'd be the Dragon Girl of the West. Yes, and maybe sharks would fly.

Belowdecks, Brine climbed into a hammock and pulled the blanket up around her ears. The cloth was scratchy and smelled of fish, like everything else on the ship. In a minute,

Peter and Tom would be down to check on her, she thought, and so she shut her eyes and pretended to sleep. She thought she heard someone laughing, but it must have been an echo from the deck above, because when she sat up to look, she couldn't see anyone.

CHAPTER 6

Magical experiments. In the interests of science, I have taken a piece of starshell. I am carrying it in my pocket along with a variety of other materials to see how long they take to corrode.

Early results:

Paper: two hours

Wood: seven hours

Gold: never

Wood from the *Onion*: never

The experiment will continue as we explore Dragon Island.

(from THOMAS GIRLING'S BOOK OF
PIRATING ADVENTURE)

Rob Grosse was supposed to be keeping watch, but he'd fallen asleep and was leaning propped against the helm. The night air was completely still, with not even the faintest breath of wind on Peter's face, and the stars were shining like tiny daggers in the sky. The only constellation Peter recognized was Orion's. The three stars that made up the mast of the mariner's ship seemed brighter than ever, as if to compensate for everything else being out of place. Peter knew the constellations changed according to where you were in the world and it was perfectly normal, but he still didn't like it.

He padded to the opposite end of the deck from Rob and sat down behind the rowing boats, where there was the least chance of anyone seeing him. It was really too dark to read but Peter opened the book he carried and peered closely at the words. Dragons. Dragons nested in isolated places, Peter read. They built nests out of gold and jewels—Peter already knew that. There were many different kinds of dragons, just like there were different kinds of fish or rabbits, but they all had scales and wings and they were all deathly dangerous. When faced with a dragon, you should run away, the book suggested—at least that way you wouldn't be looking when it killed you.

A shadow detached itself from the mast. "You're still alive," said Marfak West. The starlight shone right through him. "Congratulations."

Peter glanced up at him. "Are you planning to stand there being sarcastic all night or do you have something useful to say?"

Marfak West's ghost appeared to consider the question. "I find that sarcasm suits most circumstances. Is there anything in particular you want me to say?"

"Not really." Peter hunched lower.

The ghost's foot tapped a soundless rhythm on the deck.

"You'll never belong, you know. You're looking for a ready-made, Peter-shaped hole in the universe that you can just step into and everyone will thank you for merely existing. Trust me, it won't happen. Not anywhere, and especially not here."

Peter shook his head. That wasn't true. Just because he had a harder time fitting in anywhere than Brine or Tom— or any of the rest of the crew, come to think of it—it didn't mean he was desperate to belong. Lots of people didn't belong anywhere. Probably.

"Do you have to keep doing that?" said Peter, irritably, kicking at the ghost's foot.

Marfak West stilled and gave him a knowing grin. "If you want my advice: Stay away from that island. It's nothing but trouble."

"Why do I get the feeling you're not going to tell me what kind of trouble?" said Peter.

"Why should I?" asked the ghost. "Hopefully it will be the kind of trouble where Cassie O'Pia ends up dead. If you all die with her, it'll be a bonus."

Peter glanced over to where Rob Grosse was still snoring. "Look at it this way," he said. "If you're *really* the spirit of Marfak West, I hope you enjoy it when we all die and you find yourself surrounded by a lot of very angry ghosts. Ghosts who didn't like you much when they were alive. Of course, if you stopped sulking and helped us, that might not happen."

The shadows around Marfak West flickered. "You think you're so terribly clever, being alive, don't you?"

"It's cleverer than being dead." Peter grinned at him. "So, are you going to help us?"

The ghost began to fade. "We'll see. Your friend is right about dragons, by the way. You should look after them." He vanished.

Peter stared into the empty space where the magician's ghost had been. Look after *them*, he'd said—*them* meant more than one. Would they really find more dragons here? Peter knew you shouldn't hope for things, because hoping meant you ended up disappointed most of the time, but right now, with the island in front of him, he couldn't help himself. He hoped for dragons.

Boswell and Zen came tearing across the deck, chasing each other. Peter tried to imagine Boswell being deathly dangerous, and the thought made him smile. But, dangerous or not, Boswell was twice the size of the cat now. His wings kept getting in the way as he ran. A dragon didn't belong on a ship, Peter thought, and an ache started up in his chest. Boswell needed room to grow and more dragons to play with.

Zen crashed into Rob, waking him. Peter stood up quickly. "How far now?" He didn't want the pirate to start wondering what he was doing out here. He'd already tried telling Brine and Tom about Marfak West and they hadn't believed him. Peter didn't expect he'd do any better with Rob.

Rob studied him for a moment then shrugged. "We'll be there by morning. You can help me keep a lookout if you like?"

And so, as dawn raced across the sky some hours later, Peter was the first to see the flying castle.

It was only a small castle—one square tower with battlements and corner turrets—but it looked exceptionally solid and heavy as it floated, suspended over the highest mountain peak. Yellow smoke drifted around its base, making it look like it was sitting on a cloud.

"That's Orion's Keep?" said Cassie, using the end of her telescope to scratch her head. "It really flies. I thought Tom's books were exaggerating. Does science have an explanation for this?"

Tom shook his head. "Science is baffled. You'd better ask magic."

"Magic is equally baffled," said Peter. He'd been gazing at the castle while everyone else had gathered on deck, and he was still waiting for it to either dissolve like a mirage or crash to the ground. He could lift things into the air with magic, but not a whole castle, and not for very long. The person doing this must be the most powerful magician ever—more powerful even than Marfak West.

He shivered at the thought and tore his gaze away. "Brine, don't you remember it at all? You'd think you'd remember a flying castle."

Brine shook her head. "I don't know," she said.

Tom combed his fingers through his hair. "It might be new?"

Cassie passed her telescope to Ewan. He took one look and turned away, scowling as if the flying castle had offended his sense of reality. Bill Lightning snatched the telescope and gazed through it, one hand on his sword. Trudi chewed the ends of her hair worriedly. Boswell crept in between the two remaining rowing boats and refused to come out even when Zen pounced on his tail.

"Well," said Cassie, breaking the silence at last. "This is what we came to see. Ewan, let down the anchor."

While the crew made preparations, Peter sat down at the back of the deck with Brine. Neither of them had much to prepare. Peter thought about taking a piece of starshell with him just in case, but decided against it. If he took starshell, he knew what would happen: The first time they got into trouble—and they *would* get into trouble, because Cassie attracted trouble like a lamp attracts flying mothfish—everyone would expect him to cast a spell, and he'd be Peter the magician all over again. He still hadn't found out what he could do without magic, and this unexplored island, full of possibility, would give him that chance.

Trudi came over, holding a plate in each hand. "I made this specially. You'll need to keep your strength up today."

Peter looked at the square of bread with an egg sliding sideways off it. He picked a strand of crispy black off the yolk. "This isn't spider leg, is it?"

"I'm not sure what it is—it was in the pan already."

Peter tried the egg. It wasn't too bad, although he really didn't feel like eating anything. "Are you going to tell me what's wrong?" asked Brine. "And don't say 'nothing,' because your face has 'something is wrong' written all over it."

If that was the case, Brine's face had "everything is wrong" written on it. And "don't you dare ask about it," in even bigger letters. Peter lifted his legs to let Zen and Boswell run underneath. "Why should anything be wrong? You're about to go home. It's what you've always wanted. You'll find your family and you'll settle down while the rest of us sail on."

Brine flicked a globule of undercooked egg white at him. "Is that it? You think I'll leave the *Onion*?"

"Won't you?" asked Peter, wiping egg off his shirt. "If you find your family here, of course you'll stay with them. Don't tell me you haven't been thinking about it."

He'd never been close to his own family—his parents had sold him to Tallis Magus as soon as they discovered he could sense magic, and Peter had rarely seen them after that. If he ever found himself back in the Minutes Island cluster, he might call in to say hello, but he'd never travel across the world to find them like Brine had.

Brine dropped her gaze to her plate. "Of course I've been

thinking about it," she said. "But I don't know. I still can't remember anything. I don't know what I'll find on the island, so it's hard to make a plan right now."

And it was even harder for Brine not to make plans, Peter thought. Brine always had a plan.

"We should try the castle first," he said, scooping up the last of his egg. A trickle of warm yolk oozed down his chin. "We're looking for dragons, too, remember, and a flying castle is a good place to start."

"No!" Brine banged her plate down so hard that bits of egg went flying.

Peter brushed egg off his pants. "Um, Brine?"

She sat back and scraped her hands through her hair, laughing unsteadily. "Sorry," she said. "I slipped."

And sheep could fly and Marfak West was a nice person after all, Peter thought. "On second thought," he said, "let's explore the island first. The castle can wait."

"That sounds best," agreed Brine, and the tense lines of her face relaxed a little.

It wasn't best at all, though. Someone who could keep a whole castle in the air without it falling apart must have noticed the *Onion* by now and could already be planning an attack. The best plan would be to get up there straight-away—assuming they could find a way. Getting into the castle itself was likely to require magic, and even if Peter hadn't given up magic, he doubted he could do it. He'd levitated packing crates, but people were different: They had a habit of wriggling about, for a start, which made holding them more difficult, and if you dropped them . . .

"There's Tom," said Brine.

Peter dragged his thoughts away from dropped pirates.

Tom came out from belowdecks, wearing a hat that flopped over his eyes and carrying his messenger gull, two water bottles, and a pack so full that it looked like it was about to explode all over the deck.

"Are you sure we're going to need all that?" asked Peter.

"We don't know what we're going to need. That's the whole point," replied Tom.

"Leave the gull," said Cassie, walking up behind. "We might need to run away, and carrying a birdcage won't help."

Peter turned to look at her and his mouth fell open. Cassie always dressed up when she went ashore, and today's outfit was extravagant even by her own standards. Leather trousers, not one but two frilly shirts—one white and one red—and a pair of dark-purple boots that came up over her knees with black ribbon laces drifting in the breeze.

"Shouldn't we—um—try to draw less attention?" asked Peter. "We don't know what we're going to find here, after all."

"All the more reason to make a good first impression," said Cassie. She scratched a hand under her hat. "When we're done here, though, I'm going to invent pirate clothes for hot weather. I'm sweating already. I hope the islanders don't mind." She flashed him a smile, bright as a knife. "Are you taking any starshell?"

Peter shook his head, his fists curled in his pockets. The starshell in his palm throbbed sharply. Cassie continued to look at him, as if she thought he'd change his mind if she stared long enough, and Peter felt his cheeks growing hot. But then Boswell wandered over and stuck his claws in Cassie's knee. She yelped.

"He didn't mean it," said Peter, scooping the dragon up.

Cassie examined a hole in her trousers. "It could be worse. He'd better stay here while we explore the island. Tim Burre can look after him."

"How come they're going and not me?" grumbled Tim Burre.

"Because Brine used to live here," said Cassie, "and we'll need Tom to write down what we find. And Peter . . . well . . . Peter will be useful, too."

She could have tried to sound like she meant it, Peter thought. At least, though, she seemed to have forgotten about the starshell.

But, as he climbed into the rowing boat, he in turn wondered what he was doing. A magician without starshell. What exactly *could* he do? He glanced back at the *Onion* and thought he saw a tall, almost transparent figure waving at him, and despite the heat, he shivered.

D o you get the feeling this island doesn't like us?" asked Ewan. They'd taken both the surviving boats—Cassie, Ewan, Peter, and Brine in one, and Tom, Bill, Rob, and Trudi in the other. Ewan rowed steadily. He'd dressed up for the island, too, which meant he'd put on a shirt that didn't have holes, and his belt bristled with daggers.

Cassie tipped her hat back and watched the shore approach. "It's an island. I don't expect it cares much one way or the other."

Brine's face was fixed in a bright, worried smile and she held her sword across her knees, gripping it with both hands. Ewan Hughes had given them all fighting lessons and Brine was best—the only one of them who was any good at all, really. Tom held a sword like it was a pen, and Peter was always too worried he'd actually hit someone, even though Ewan assured him the chances of that were roughly the same as fish growing legs.

The boat nosed into the sand at the water's edge. Cassie jumped straight out and drew her cutlass. Peter helped Ewan drag the boat farther up the shore, and looked for somewhere to tie it. He didn't like the look of the trees—their trunks were twisted in odd shapes, and the moss that patched their branches looked like fur.

Tom bent down and scooped up a handful of yellow sand. "It glitters," he said.

Small flecks of gold caught the sunlight. Peter grinned. "Gold. Gold means dragons, doesn't it? Let's go look for them."

Cassie put her cutlass away. "We'll split into two parties. Ewan, Trudi, and Brine, you're with me. Rob, Bill, Tom, and Peter, you're in charge of guarding the boats here until we return."

She spoke so briskly that it took a moment or two for Peter to realize what she'd said. His grin froze.

Tom threw his pack down. "That's not fair!"

Rob Grosse scowled and folded his arms. "I didn't row all the way here just so I could babysit a boat!"

"You didn't row—I did," said Trudi with the smugness of someone who knew she was in the exploring party. "We're down to our last two boats thanks to all of you. What if they get stolen by marauding islanders while we're all off exploring?"

"You stay behind, then, if you're so worried," growled Rob.

Trudi's cheeks turned pink. "We need supplies. I have to look around and decide whether anything here is safe to eat."

Peter walked past Cassie to the boats and sat down. When Cassie got an idea in her head, a herd of rhinocerbeast wouldn't shift it. Arguing with her was a waste of time. Besides, he had the start of an idea—a plan, even.

"Fine," he said loudly, avoiding Brine's gaze. "We'll stay here. I bet you won't find anything interesting anyway."

Brine dug her toes into the sand. Cassie gave Peter a narrow look and he ducked his head, wondering if she'd guessed what he was thinking. But Trudi and Ewan were already starting eagerly toward the trees.

"Rob and Bill, stay here," said Cassie. "That's an order. Right, let's go and explore. And, Brine, try to look like you're enjoying yourself. This is an adventure."

CHAPTER 7

The first rule of adventuring is: Be Prepared. Be prepared to
fight. Be prepared to run. Be prepared for anything.

(from BRINE SEABORNE'S BOOK OF PLANS)

Brine didn't say anything as she followed Cassie into the
trees. There wasn't much point arguing with Cassie, for a
start. And, besides, Brine had seen the look in Peter's eyes as
he'd sat down: He wasn't going to stay meekly on the beach.
She just hoped he didn't find dragons before she did. She
tripped on a knot of grass and narrowly avoided landing in a
bramble patch.

"So, what's the plan?" she asked, slapping away several
large, bright-blue flies. "Stumble about until we're eaten alive
by insects?"

"Unless we're eaten alive by dragons first," said Cassie
cheerfully. "You're the chief planner. What do you think?"

Brine slapped more flies away. "I don't know? I suppose
we could look around and see what's here, and run away fast
if we get into trouble."

"Sounds like a good plan," said Cassie.

Brine tried to ignore the hammering in her chest. She'd never known Cassie to be cautious before. They were pirates: They didn't run away from trouble; they caused it. With cutlasses, usually. She gripped her sword hilt, trying to feel like a pirate, but her fingers were stuck together with sweat, and the cloud of insects above her head kept growing.

The branches above her rustled, and she looked up in time to see a brown tail disappearing into the canopy of leaves. Not a dragon—it had hair, not scales. Still, it was her first glimpse of an animal on Dragon Island.

"It's too quiet," complained Ewan a moment later. "I don't like it."

"I'd be quiet if a bunch of well-dressed strangers were tramping over my island," said Cassie.

"No, you wouldn't," said Ewan. "You'd rush out yelling and waving something sharp and pointy. The only reason you'd be quiet is if you were planning an ambush . . . not that you ever plan."

"We have a plan now, don't we?" Cassie said pointedly. "Brine thought of one. We look around and run away if there's trouble."

Brine walked on, listening to them bicker. Every rustle, every snap of a twig sounded like someone lying in wait and, with every second that passed, Brine was less eager to meet them. She'd been six years old when she was found in the Atlas Ocean on the other side of the world and, until a few months ago, she hadn't left the island cluster of Minutes. She only had Marfak West's word that this was her home. What if he'd lied—or worse, what if he'd told the truth but no one here remembered her or wanted her back? She'd been gone for over three years, after all.

"Mushrooms!" exclaimed Trudi, pointing to some bulging red-and-white stalks. "I wonder if they're edible?"

Brine pulled the pirate along before Trudi could decide to find out. Then she heard another sound, on and off through the trees. She recognized it at once because she lived with it every day—the rush of water. She paused. "Listen."

Cassie and Ewan were still arguing about how they'd plan an ambush. Brine threw a stick at Cassie and she leaped around, her cutlass half out.

"Will you stop that?" said Brine. "I think I can hear a river."

They all paused. For a second or two Brine forgot about the sticky heat, the bramble scratches, and the annoying insects still circling around her head.

"Do dragons live by rivers?" asked Trudi.

Cassie pushed her cutlass home. "I don't know, but people do. Come on."

They hurried on, walking faster. The ground soon began to slope downward and the undergrowth thinned, becoming patchy with more clusters of mushrooms and even some yellow flowers raising their faces to the light. The trees changed, too, the lumpy, moss-covered trunks giving way to a collection of slender trees with pale bark and long golden leaves that rustled like paper in the wind.

Then they found the river. It appeared so suddenly in front of them that Brine would have fallen into it if Ewan hadn't caught hold of her. They all stood and looked down at the fast-flowing water as it rushed over rocks and fallen trees before dipping sharply into a waterfall. A cool haze filled the air and made Brine feel like she was seeing through Mirrormist.

"This water is fresh," said Trudi, crouching next to the bank. "We should have brought barrels."

"If you want to drag barrels through the jungle, you can do it on your own," said Cassie. She clambered down over rocks. "There's a path here."

By "path" she meant a jumble of rocks with occasional flat places where you could just about fit one foot or the other. But the others were already climbing down, and Brine could either follow or stay at the top by herself. She followed, holding on to rocks with her hands as she went. Water thundered past and spread out into a large lake at the bottom of the fall. No sign of dragons—or of people, come to think of it.

Trudi squatted down beside the lake and sank her arms into the water. "It goes down a long way."

A few bubbles rose to the surface in the middle of the lake. Brine's flesh prickled. She didn't know why, but something was making her afraid. "Trudi, wait." She slid down the last few rocks to join the others. The ground around them was soft and covered in marks—footprints. Some were human, and Brine's pulse quickened. Others were animal—tiny ones that looked like birds, and a few that were much bigger.

Much, much bigger.

"Trudi, get away from the lake," said Brine.

Trudi ignored her, reached a little farther, and then fell in with a splash. Brine started forward, but Trudi stood up, laughing.

"It's fine," she said. "It's actually quite warm." She paused. "Hold on. I think I've found something."

She bent and pulled a long, brown body out of the water.

Cassie whipped out her sword. "It's a snake!"

But Trudi kept pulling and more snake emerged. If it was a snake, it was the biggest one Brine had ever seen. Its body should have ended in a head by now, but it just kept getting thicker.

"What *is* that?" asked Ewan. "It looks more like a . . ." He tailed off, appropriately enough.

The thing in Trudi's hands wasn't a snake; it was part of something much bigger. Brine stood, frozen in panic. Her legs couldn't decide whether to run away or to charge into the lake after Trudi.

Cassie took a step forward. "I think you should come out now," she said, her voice as flat and calm as the lake had been.

The tail twitched in Trudi's hands then snapped out of her grip and lashed backward at her. She fell over with a splash, flailing water in all directions as she windmilled her arms.

Cassie and Ewan shouted and rushed into the water. And Brine yelled because she saw the thing that was rising from the center of the lake.

No wings. Brine's mind scrambled for a coherent thought, and that was the only thing it found. That meant it couldn't be a dragon. It was probably too big to be a dragon anyway. Its body was as big as a ship. They could all live in its body and have room for visitors.

Trudi scrambled up and stumbled back toward the lake edge. The monster swung its massive neck around to look at her—a neck that was longer than the trees—and started to wade out of the lake. Water poured off its sides. Brine gripped her sword hard. She didn't even remember drawing it. It felt tiny in her hand, and completely useless. She looked around to tell Peter to do something, but of course Peter wasn't there.

The monster dipped its head lower and blew out a spray of water. Its wide mouth looked like it was smiling. Happy at the prospect of eating them, Brine thought, and her hand shook so hard, she had to press her arm against her body to keep it still. The monster ignored her completely—in fact, it ignored all of them. It thundered on slowly past to the nearest group of trees and tore off a mouthful of papery leaves and branches.

Ewan lowered his cutlass and laughed. "I don't believe it. It's a plant-eater!"

The sudden relief caused Brine's legs to give way. She sat down at the edge of the lake with a thump.

"That's a first," said Cassie. "A monster that doesn't want to eat us alive." She sheathed her cutlass and wiped her forearm over her face. "First a sea-monster made of plants, and now a land-monster that eats plants. We should get back to the others—they are never going to believe us about this."

But then the trees rustled and parted and Brine spun around to see a second animal. This one was much smaller than the first, but on its hind legs it was taller than Cassie. For a second or two it stood still, and Brine was able to take in the sight of its mottled brown skin, the orange eyes, and its front legs, which were comically small compared to its body. There was nothing funny about its claws, though, or the way its eyes fixed on them hungrily. Brine could almost hear it thinking, *Food.*

Brine's heart rose into her throat. She stood up slowly. "I don't think this one is a plant-eater."

The monster gave a low growl. Its teeth looked like knives. The front ones had bits of meat hanging off them.

"I believe this is the part of Brine's plan where we run away fast," said Cassie.

The monster rushed at them. They ran.

CHAPTER 8

Remember: The most dangerous monsters don't always look like monsters. Sometimes they do. Actually, a lot of the time they do. Most of the time.

(from THOMAS GIRLING'S BOOK OF PIRATING ADVENTURES)

Tom turned on Peter the moment Cassie led the others into the trees. "Yes, Cassie," he said sarcastically. "Whatever you say, Cassie; we'll all sit here and do nothing, Cassie." He kicked sand at Peter. "You might not have noticed, but I was looking forward to exploring this island."

Peter sighed. "We're going to explore the island; don't worry." His gaze went back to the castle, real and solid and entirely unmirage-like halfway up the sky. A cold thrill ran through him. "Not even magic can beat gravity forever," he said.

Tom took his glasses off and scrubbed the lenses in angry circles. "What's that supposed to mean?"

"It means there's something very wrong with that castle and we should investigate." Peter took a step closer to Bill and

Rob. "I bet you anything," he said, raising his voice to make sure they could hear, "if we heard a strange noise. Over there, for example . . ." He pointed to the trees at the top of the cove. "And if we thought that, in the interests of safety, we should go and check it out, nobody is going to come running back to tell us we can't."

Rob and Bill both stared at him blankly. Peter might as well have been speaking in a foreign language. In a way, he was—he was speaking the language of disobeying Cassie.

Tom understood, though. Peter saw the sudden gleam in his eyes, the quick grin lighting up his face. He'd had a life-time of rigid rules in the libraries of Barnard's Reach, and he must have learned to bend the rules now and again.

"I didn't hear anything," said Bill.

"You're right," said Tom. "It's quiet. Suspiciously quiet." He took a few paces up the sand. "It's the kind of quiet that makes me think marauding islanders are creeping up to ambush us right this second. We should definitely do something."

Bill and Rob still didn't move. "You're pirates," said Peter. "You laugh in the face of terror, remember?"

The pirates exchanged glances. "Terror," agreed Bill. "But not Cassie. We don't laugh in the face of Cassie."

Rob nodded vigorously. "Anyone who laughs in the face of Cassie is likely to lose their head."

Honestly, at this rate Cassie would be back before they'd gone two steps. Peter shifted his feet, listening to the sand crunch. Flecks of brilliant gold shone underfoot. Gold didn't necessarily mean dragons, but if dragons didn't have access to a treasure hoard to build a nest, a mix of sand and gold might do instead. He started to walk. "Of course, if you prefer, Tom and I can have a quick look around while you wait here. Just to make sure we're not being ambushed."

He knew that Rob and Bill would never let them go off on their own, and sure enough, Rob ran after them.

Bill's gaze finally shifted to the trees and he slung his bow over his shoulder. "I suppose five minutes won't hurt. Just as long as Cassie doesn't find out."

It felt wrong to be at the front of the group and not have Brine ahead of him, but why shouldn't he take charge for once, Peter thought. Magicians were always ordering people around.

Tom took his pen out and scratched arrows on the trees as they passed. "So we can find our way back," he said.

"Good idea." Knowing they could get back to the boats if need be made him feel better. Peter walked on, stepping over thorny branches. The castle drew his gaze constantly, even through the thick ceiling of tree branches overhead, and he had to keep reminding himself to look down and keep an eye on his surroundings. The ground was sandy, spiked with shells and gray stones, and tiny, brightly colored lizards darted away from under his feet as he walked.

"If Cassie gets back before us, she won't be happy," warned Rob in a voice as grim as Tim Burre predicting the end of the world.

Peter picked a flying ant out of his ear. Really, though, did it matter if Cassie wasn't happy? Even if she found out they'd disobeyed orders—and she wouldn't because they wouldn't tell her—what was she going to do about it? She could bluster and threaten, but she couldn't make them go back in time and not go exploring.

That sort of thinking was practically mutiny. Peter panicked momentarily and blundered into a tree. He stopped still, blinking away stars.

"You all right?" asked Bill.

Peter was surprised to find that he was. He wiped his hands over his face and looked at the smears from the various squashed insects on his palms. He was disobeying Cassie, leading his own group of explorers, and nothing had gone horribly wrong. If this was Peter without the magic, he quite liked it.

Tom's pen snapped on a tree.

"How are we going to find our way now?" asked Bill.

"We'll remember it," said Peter, pretending that he hadn't just been thinking exactly the same thing. He imagined all his fear turning into a ball and shrinking smaller and smaller until it was so small and light, he could flick it away. He drew in a few breaths. A branch snapped nearby. Was that an ambush of angry villagers or just an animal? Peter didn't wait to find out. "It's a pen, not a prophecy of doom," he said. "Let's carry on."

He splashed through a stream where a rainbow of flying beetles hovered. Tom swatted at them with his notebook. "What if there are dragons, and Cassie finds them before us?"

Peter imagined Cassie in a fight with a dragon. "Cassie would never attack dragons."

Tom walked on. "Cassie knows that, but do the dragons?"

A distant roaring shook the trees. They all stopped dead, and Rob drew his sword. "What was that?"

The roaring continued. Peter's face prickled with sweat.

"The boats," said Rob.

"Tom, come on."

Tom didn't move. "I'd love to," he said. "But I think I'm stuck."

Peter looked down. The ground was soft underfoot, and sandy. He stepped back quickly, leaving footprints that were already half filled with water. The sand around Tom's feet was moving: undulating up and down like waves in slow motion, and air bubbles rose and burst. Tom tried to turn around, wobbled, and almost fell.

"I'm sinking," he said, his voice rising in panic. "Help!"

CHAPTER 9

Though you're faced with a beast that might want you deceased,
Never fear, for salvation is nigh.
As soon as they see her, brave Cassie O'Pia,
The deadliest monsters will fly.

(from THE BALLAD OF CASSIE O'PIA,
Verse 314, Author Unknown)

Brine had done a lot of running away since she'd met Cassie. They'd run from guards and librarians and invisible snow bears. All the practice meant she was becoming quite good at it, but that fact was easily outweighed by the large, angry monster right behind her.

Ewan dragged her aside just as the monster came bursting through the trees. Everyone dived in different directions, except for Cassie, who stepped out in front of it, her cutlasses drawn.

Brine swallowed a scream as the monster lunged, sure that Cassie was going to be trampled. But Cassie slipped to one side, then jumped up behind the monster and stabbed both cutlasses at its tail. It roared and turned around impossibly fast. One of Cassie's cutlasses was wrenched out of her grip. She kept hold of the other one and rolled backward as Trudi threw a rock. It bounced off the monster's head, making it forget Cassie for a second.

Cassie landed flat beside Brine. "It could be worse," she said, panting. "At least it's not turning invisible or hypnotizing us. You want to try running again?"

"Yes, please," said Brine.

They fled, Ewan running backward to throw knives. Branches slapped across Brine's face, and she put her arms over her head and stumbled on. Every branch on the ground seemed to be lying in wait to trip her up, but Cassie's firm hand on her back kept her going.

"Straight ahead," said Cassie. "Don't stop." Giving Brine a final shove, she wheeled around and sprinted off away from her.

Brine crashed to a halt. "You're going the wrong way!"

"Get to the boats!" Cassie called, still running. The monster paused for a second, swinging its head from side to side as if deciding who to attack. Cassie hurled a tree branch at it, and the monster roared and charged after her.

"Do as she says!" snapped Ewan, and he and Trudi took off in pursuit.

Brine stood frozen in shock. And then, before her

scrambled thoughts could get any orders to her legs, she saw Cassie suddenly falter, flail at thin air, and then vanish into the ground.

Brine screamed. "Cassie!"

The monster appeared to hear her, and it turned its head, but then its feet hit the same patch of ground and it, too, disappeared.

Run, Brine thought furiously. *Stupid legs. Run!*

Somehow, she got moving again and she tore after Ewan and Trudi. Ewan put out a hand to hold her back, and she slammed straight into him. When she saw what had happened, she let out a cry.

Cassie had fallen into a pit. Large enough to hold several monsters and deep enough to keep them there. For a few awfully long seconds, Brine thought Cassie must be dead, and her vision turned hot with tears. But then she saw the pirate captain clinging to a branch sticking out near the top. The monster snarled right below her, snapping at her purple boots.

Trudi grabbed a branch off the ground and waved it around the opposite side of the pit. "Nice monster. Come to Trudi!" She threw the branch at it and reached back for another one. The monster gave a low growl and leaped at her.

Ewan leaned over the side of the pit and stretched out toward Cassie. Kneeling at the edge of the pit, Brine could only watch, and she'd never felt so useless before.

Cassie reached up and caught hold of Ewan's hand, but at

the same moment, Brine saw the monster turn and prepare to jump.

"Look out!" she cried.

The monster launched itself at Cassie's legs with a roar. She kicked it hard in the face, and it let her go just long enough for Ewan to haul Cassie out of the way. She scrambled out of the pit and collapsed flat next to Brine. Her boots were shredded, and blood seeped through her trouser legs.

For a few seconds, no one spoke.

Cassie sat up. "Those were my best boots."

"You're hurt," said Brine. Her throat felt tight and hot. Something stung the back of her neck.

"Stupid insects," said Trudi, slapping at herself. Then she staggered.

Brine blinked as the trees around her blurred and turned into a shimmering block of green. Through the haze, she saw Cassie start to her feet then fall back down, and then a pair of shapes came sweeping through the trees. Flying monsters with faces like rats and silver rings around their ankles. They shrieked and plunged into the pit, and the ground trembled with a renewed storm of roaring and screaming.

Dragons, Brine thought—they'd found their dragons.

"Peter, do something," she said, but of course Peter wasn't there.

The world turned black.

After all the running and shouting, it felt almost peaceful.

CHAPTER 10

The language of the eight oceans is called Oceanic. Some people speak it with strange accents, others have their own versions and dialects, but essentially it is the same wherever you go. Remember, however, that just because someone speaks your language, it doesn't mean they are friendly.

(from ALDEBRAN BOSWELL'S BOOK OF THE WORLD)

Peter, do something," said Tom. His voice quavered. He was sinking fast, the sand already lapping at his knees.

Rob held Peter back. "Careful," he warned, "or you'll end up in there with him. Tom, there's nothing to worry about— it's only sinksand. We've all fallen in a hundred times. We'll get you out now; just don't move. Moving makes you sink faster."

"I'm already sinking faster," said Tom, but he stopped wriggling. He dug in a few pockets and found his notebook, which he threw to Peter. "Look after that. Don't read it—it's private."

Only a librarian could care about a book while drowning in sinksand. Peter had no intention of reading it, but he pretended to look anyway. "What about if you die," he joked. "Can I read it then?"

Tom's face crimsoned. "If you read that book, I'll come back and haunt you."

"You'll have to get in line," said Peter. Something rustled nearby in the trees and he looked around nervously. Could Marfak West follow him onto the island? He hoped not, but who knew what ghosts could and couldn't do?

"Out of the way, Peter," said Bill. The pirate picked up a vine that was snaking across the ground by Peter's feet and tossed it to Tom. "Here. Wrap this around your waist and hang on."

Peter stepped back out of the way. It seemed that Rob and Bill knew what they were doing. It was almost disappointing that he wouldn't be able to leap in and save the day.

Tom looped the vine around his waist. "Ready," he said. Then his eyes widened. "No. Not ready. It's hurting me! Get it off me!"

The sand thrashed as if it were alive. Bill dropped the vine with a yell. "It bit me!"

Peter stared at the blood dripping from Bill's hand. Then he felt something crawling over his feet.

Vines. Horrible, slimy vines, all of them full of dark spines and little crimson suckers that opened and shut like hungry mouths. Some of them burrowed into the ground where Bill's blood had dripped, writhing together as they fought over the droplets.

"Ugh!" said Peter, and tore his foot free. This was worse than spiders.

More vines slithered into the sand where Tom floundered.

"Help!" he yelled, his voice full of panic. "They're eating me!"

Peter dragged his feet free of vines. "Keep back," ordered Rob. "You won't help by getting stuck as well."

"But he's sinking!" Peter struggled in the pirate's grip. "I should never have left my starshell on the *Onion*. We always get into trouble."

Vines snapped at his legs. Meanwhile, just two paces out of reach, Tom was waist deep in sand and a vine was trying to wrap around his neck. Peter watched helplessly. He'd wanted to see what he could do without magic, and here was the answer. Nothing.

Tom wrenched a hand free. "Peter, catch!"

He threw something round and gray at him. Peter missed it and bent down to retrieve it. It was a rolled-up sock, or the remains of a sock. Three-quarters of it had worn away, and the remaining bits were unraveling. Peter felt the starshell even before he'd uncovered it; the magic thumped against his hand and made his skin fizz.

"I was doing some experiments," said Tom. "Sorry. I should have asked first, but I knew you'd say no. Ow," he added as a vine wormed into his sleeve.

Peter gripped the starshell tightly. Magic filled his hand, warm and comforting and familiar. The tight panic left him, and he drew in a breath and slowly released it. Then he raised his hand to draw the spellshape . . .

An arrow thudded into the ground. One of the vines holding Tom whipped away from him and fell limply onto the sand.

Cassie, Peter thought. His hand dropped, his whole body shaking. Cassie had come looking for them and found them just in time.

"It's my fault," he began as the branches parted. "I wanted—"

The words shriveled and died in his throat. It wasn't Cassie who stepped out of the trees, but a girl. Dark-skinned and crinkly-haired—she looked a bit like Brine. An older, scowlier version of Brine, with a bow in one hand, a long knife in the other, and a rope coiled around her waist.

"Who . . . ?" said Peter. He couldn't speak. He wheezed air into his lungs and pushed the starshell into his pocket, embarrassingly aware that his cheeks were flaming hot.

The girl ignored him and stabbed her knife into the ground several times. The vines hissed like snakes and a couple of them darted at her, but she stamped on them and they withdrew into the ground. In a moment Tom was free. The girl threw him her rope. Tom caught it and flopped flat on his face as she pulled. He burbled something unintelligible, his face full of sand, and then his legs came free with a sound like a ship tearing away from octopus suckers. He collapsed onto solid ground, groaning loudly.

"Are you hurt?" asked Bill.

"No, just squashed and stung and covered in sand. Which tastes horrible, by the way."

"Well, that's why people don't normally eat sand," said Peter. He held his hand out to the girl. "Thank you. I'm Peter. These are my friends, Bill, Rob, and Tom."

The girl looked at his outstretched hand as if she was wondering whether to shake it or cut it off.

Maybe she didn't speak Oceanic, Peter thought. He jabbed himself in the chest. "Peter. Me Peee-ter."

She sighed and started to coil up her rope. "I heard you the first time," she said. "I'm Stella. You're from the ship, aren't you? What's wrong with your skin?"

"My skin?" Alarm mingled with embarrassment. Had the starshell started corroding him? He looked at his hands and couldn't see anything wrong.

"It's white," said Stella. "Are you ill?"

Tom got up. "No one comes here, remember. They're all afraid of falling off the edge of the world." He combed sand out of his hair with his fingers and addressed Stella. "Lots of people have white skin where we come from."

Stella peered at him. "Really? Why?"

Peter's cheeks smarted. Cassie would have handled this differently. Cassie would have made some joke, and she and Stella would be laughing together already like they were long-lost friends.

Stella kicked the end of a vine. "These are sandvines. They

grow around sinksand. They wait until something falls in and then they go for you. When you're sinking, it's normal to grab for anything you can, but once the vines get hold of you they won't let go. They pull you under the sand so you drown and then they eat you—slowly."

Tom looked green under his coating of drying sand. "Um, thanks for pulling me out."

"Next time, aim for the ground where they're rooted," said Stella. "They root themselves into anything, even stone, but the roots never go deep and if you cut them, the vines die."

"Next time, I think I won't walk into sinksand," said Tom.

Stella nodded. "That would work, too."

Tom pushed his hair back and started emptying sand out of his pockets. If they waited for him to finish, they'd be here all day, Peter thought. "We should go back to the boats," he said. "Before the others find us gone—or anything else tries to kill us."

Stella turned to look at the trees. "There are more of you? I wondered what disturbed the dinosaurs."

Peter didn't know the word, but it didn't sound good. "Are dinosaurs like dragons?"

The girl gave a snort of laughter. "No, because dinosaurs are real and dragons are just a story."

Tom stared back at the sinksand. Rob and Bill made a show of studying the trees around them.

"Maybe they're just hiding," suggested Bill after a pause.

Stella rolled her eyes. "How have you people managed to stay alive this long?"

"Luck," said Peter. He shook his head. He wasn't giving up on dragons yet. They'd all been so sure they would find dragons here—even Ewan, who didn't usually believe in something until it was trying to eat him. "Who else lives here?" he asked. Maybe they could talk to someone older, someone who remembered them.

"There's the village. And the castle, but you don't want to go there. That's all. Nobody goes far from home because it's dangerous. I'm not really supposed to be out here now."

That made five of them, Peter thought. They should start a club.

"Why are you here, then?" asked Tom. He sneezed. "Not that I'm complaining."

Stella regarded him coolly. "It's none of your business."

It was so much the sort of thing that Brine would say that Peter grinned. He kicked a vine out of the way and stepped back from it as it squirmed. Now that he knew how to handle them, they didn't seem so bad. "If the village is the only place on the island with people, the others may have already found it. Or the village will have found them. Given how Cassie and Ewan normally charge about attracting attention." He turned to Stella and smiled. Cassie was always smiling at people, and it seemed to work for her. "I think you should take us to the village. We'll tell you all about our home, and you can tell us about dinosaurs and dragons."

"What makes you think I want to hear about your home?" asked Stella.

Peter kept smiling. Stella dropped her gaze and blew out a sigh. "I suppose you can come if you like. If your friends have been causing trouble, Marapi will have noticed."

"Who's Marapi?" asked Peter, but Stella was already walking away. Peter glanced at the others, but they all seemed to be waiting for him to decide. He wasn't sure he wanted to be in charge, but someone had to do it, so he shrugged and followed.

CHAPTER 11

There are some things you cannot plan for. Being taken captive by hostile islanders, for example. If you find yourself in that situation, the best you can do is try to stay alive. Alive, you can always do something later. Being dead tends to cut down on your options.

(from BRINE SEABORNE'S BOOK OF PLANS)

Brine wondered how the world had managed to turn itself sideways. She'd only just opened her eyes, so she knew she must be lying down, but the sky was made of brown dirt, and something narrow dug into the whole length of her back and made her hands hurt. She blinked a few times and, gradually, the world put itself back together and resembled something approaching reality.

The reality didn't look good. Brine wasn't lying, but standing, tied fast to some kind of pole or post, and her head was hanging forward, so all she could see was the ground between her feet. Her mouth tasted of dirt. What had happened? She remembered running through the jungle with a monster on her heels, but then it all got muddled. Cassie had fallen, and then . . .

"Dragons!" Brine shouted and jerked her head up, smacking it into the post behind her. She heard people laughing as her vision swam. She shut her eyes, then tried opening them again slowly.

People in a semicircle around her. People with skin as dark as her own, which caused Brine's heart to lift—until she saw their spears, and the way they watched her as if they were waiting to throw them at her. A pile of knives and cutlasses lay on the ground—the pirates' weapons. Brine turned her head carefully from side to side and saw Cassie, Ewan, and Trudi, all tied to posts. Weaponless but alive. They wouldn't be tied up if they weren't alive. Relief came bubbling out of her.

"Cassie," she whispered.

Cassie lifted her head a fraction but didn't answer. Brine wasn't sure she'd even heard her. She cast her gaze past the people to the circle of huts and the high wall that circled them. The wall looked like it had been built out of tree trunks, and it was far too high for Brine to climb even if she could break free and run, which she doubted.

But then she saw the dragons. Four of them were perched on rooftops, watching her. But they were as unlike Boswell as Brine could imagine. Boswell's scales were a shifting mix of green and silver, like the sea, but these dragons were dull gray, the color of wet clay, and their faces were far too long, ending in curved beaks. Part dragon, part bat, part bird.

While she was looking, the crowd around Brine parted, and a woman walked through. Her left eye was missing, replaced by an angry red scar that ran diagonally from the middle of her forehead to the ragged remains of her ear. Despite this, she stood straight-backed and didn't take her one-eyed gaze off Brine, ignoring the shuffling and muttering that came from behind her.

Brine's mind scrambled for a plan, failed to find one, and then gave up working altogether. "Are those dragons?" Of all the questions she could ask upon regaining consciousness tied to a stake, that was probably not the most useful.

The woman smiled and the people around her murmured. Brine wasn't sure whether it was in surprise that she could speak or anticipation at the prospect of killing her.

"They are called teradons," the woman said. "You speak Apcaron, then." A cutlass hung at her side—Cassie's cutlass, Brine thought, recognizing it. Cassie was not going to be happy about that when she woke up.

"What's Apcaron?" asked Brine. "Who are you?"

The woman's single eye narrowed to a slit. "I don't know how you do things where you come from, but you are our prisoners. You will answer questions, and you will refrain from asking any more. Is that clear?"

Brine nodded, her mouth dry.

The woman smiled again, the scars creasing on her face. "Good. My name is Marapi, ruler of Apcaron Island. You can start by telling me who you are, what you're doing here, and why we shouldn't kill you."

How do you know she's not leading us into a trap?" whispered Tom.

Peter watched Stella chop her way through a patch of foliage. "Why would she lead us into a trap?"

"It's what they do on forgotten islands like this. I've read about them—my mother was the Assistant Keeper of Geography, remember. They're all full of people who appear friendly and then try to stuff you into a cooking pot."

Bill and Rob both nodded in agreement. "A cooking pot as big as a house," added Bill. "With flames so hot you'd roast your eyes just by looking."

Peter sighed.

Stella looked back. "If I wanted to eat anyone, I wouldn't choose you. You're too dirty and covered in ink."

Peter pushed on after her. "You mentioned someone called Marapi. Who is he?"

Stella slowed. "Marapi isn't a he. She's my father's sister." She slashed through a branch, scowling. "My father, Cerro, is the leader of Apcaron Island, but Marapi is older than him, so she thinks she ought to be in charge. She's always causing him trouble. Then, last year, a dinosaur attacked her and she nearly died. She said it proved the island isn't safe, and that if

Cerro can't protect us, he isn't fit to lead. She persuaded the people to build a big wall around the village to keep the dinosaurs out, and she doesn't let anyone leave now unless it's in one of her hunting parties. Which I'm not in."

"So what are you doing out here?" asked Tom, ducking under a branch.

"Nothing. Just getting away for a while."

Peter slowed. "Why doesn't your father do something? If he's the leader, can't he just tell her to stop?"

"Not anymore." Stella struck a branch, making it swing back hard into Peter's face. "Marapi's got him locked up. I have a brother—his name's Ren and he's only six years old. Marapi gave him to Orion's Keep. She said she did it to keep him safe, because Cerro wasn't looking after him properly. But everyone knows she swapped him for spellstones."

"Spellstones?" Peter asked.

"Yes, you know—magic. I think Marapi expected Cerro to argue about it for a while and then give up. Instead, we tried to rescue him. Only it went wrong. We escaped. But we didn't get Ren, and Cerro was hurt—both his legs broken. Marapi accused him of putting the village in danger—we need the magicians' spellstones. She's kept Cerro locked up since. And now people are starting to say he won't walk again anyway, so Marapi should just take over."

Peter's gaze drifted up. He couldn't see the castle through the patchwork of branches overhead, but he could feel it: cold and heavy. He slid his hand into his pocket and felt the piece of starshell there. The warmth of magic against his fingers steadied him. "How many magicians are in Orion's Keep?" he asked.

"Magi, you mean. Three—there are three of them."

Three didn't sound too bad. Three magicians against a whole ship of pirates. It depended how powerful the magicians were, of course, but if they were using a lot of their magic to keep the castle airborne, they might not have much to spare for fighting. "We can help," said Peter.

Stella laughed. "You couldn't even stay out of sinksand."

"You haven't met Cassie yet," said Rob. "Cassie's good at rescuing people. And we're going to go to the castle anyway, so we might as well do some rescuing while we're there. Where is this village of yours?"

Stella pointed through the trees. "We're nearly there."

>+++++++●

Apcaron. The word was completely new to Brine, yet it sent a spear of cold through her. It made her think of stones and darkness and a feeling of being suffocated. She wished Cassie were awake, but Cassie stood, tied fast to the post, her head dangling, and she didn't open her eyes. Her bare feet were stained with a mix of dirt and blood.

Stay calm, Brine instructed herself. They were all still alive, and that meant things could get better.

Her head thumped. She'd imagined many times over what it would be like to come home, but none of her imaginings had ever been like this. She wriggled her hands behind her until her fingers found a knot in the rope. If she could just work it undone . . . "My name is Brine Seaborne—or it is now. I was found on the other side of the world, and I can't remember anything that happened before that, but I think I came from here."

A few people around murmured in surprise and a few of them put down their spears, but Marapi shook her head. "Nobody leaves Apcaron." She gestured at Cassie, Trudi, and Ewan. "Who are these? Your servants?"

"No, they're my friends." Brine struggled in frustration. Why did they have to tie these knots so tightly?

"Actually," said Cassie, opening her eyes suddenly, staring straight at Marapi, "I'm her captain. Her *angry* captain. Poisoning people is cowardly, and if there's one thing I hate, it's cowards. And large monsters." She shifted her feet, leaving red footprints in the sand. "I advise you to let us go before you become very sorry."

It was strange how the world could be exactly the same and yet completely different. Brine was still tied to the stake; sweat still dribbled down her face. But Cassie was awake and back in charge and so everything was all right again. She wasn't sure how it would be yet, but Cassie would think of something.

Marapi swung Cassie's cutlass, still staring at Brine. "If you're traveling with foreigners, you have very bad judgment. I shouldn't expect a child to know better." She made the world *child* sound like an insult.

Brine struggled harder. "I'm not a child. I'm twelve years old—nearly thirteen—and I'm looking for my family. Somebody must remember me."

"Foreigners are inferior," said Marapi. "And you're a liar. Once again, who are you and what do you really want here? Or shall I feed you to the teradons?"

This was like Marfak West all over again, Brine thought, and a sudden surge of rage caught her by surprise. She'd sailed here from the other side of the world, and for what? To be eaten alive by insects, chased by monsters, and now tied up and threatened by a woman who was determined not to believe her.

"All right," said Brine, "I'll tell you who I am." She pulled herself up straight against the stake, no longer struggling. "I am Brine Seaborne, pulled out of the waves to start my life over again. Once I was a magician's servant, and now I am the friend of pirates and the rescuer of dragons. And this . . ." Her voice trembled then steadied. "This is Cassie O'Pia, captain of the pirate ship *Onion*. She's the most famous pirate in the world. She defeated the Dreaded Great Sea Beast of the South; she saved the Columba Islands from the plague. She braved the storms of the dead and battled monsters in the ice plains at the top of the world. She defeated the evilest magician on the eight oceans, and she saved the libraries of Barnard's Reach with their thousands of years of stories."

Brine's voice rose. It almost felt as if someone else was speaking and she was just opening and shutting her mouth in time with the words. Cassie was grinning next to her, and Ewan and Trudi had both opened their eyes and were listening and nodding along to the story. Brine met Marapi's gaze and smiled. "Cassie O'Pia is stronger than anyone else," she said, "and braver than anyone else, and it doesn't matter what trouble we're in, because she always finds a way out."

Marapi raised Cassie's cutlass and stepped toward her. "Not this time."

Maybe she intended to kill them, or maybe she was going to cut them free. Brine never found out, because something huge burst through the village wall and everyone started screaming and running.

CHAPTER 12

The key to good planning is preparation. Always find out as much about the enemy as possible. Also, be prepared to find out that they're not really the enemy.

(from THOMAS GIRLING'S BOOK OF PIRATING ADVENTURES)

It took Peter a moment to see that the trees in front weren't trees—not anymore. They'd been cut and placed together to form a wall that stretched out to either side as far as he could see. He crept close and peered through a gap.

He saw huts, and a crowd of people standing around four posts. Each post had someone tied to it. He was too far away to see who they were, but he didn't need to see—he knew it was Brine and the others.

"I knew we shouldn't have left the boats," said Rob, drawing his sword.

Peter stopped him. "Wait. We can't just go charging in there."

"Why not?"

"Because . . ." Peter didn't know.

"Because there are hundreds of people in there and we can't attack them all," said Tom sensibly. "We need a plan. A plan that doesn't just involve hitting people."

They needed more than a plan, Peter thought. They needed magic. His starshell dug into his leg, making his skin prickle. A bird, or something, screeched overhead, and he looked up to see dark wings.

"Teradons," said Stella. "Flying dinosaurs. We use them for hunting." She watched the creature circling, her hands on her hips. "You'd better wait here, and I'll go in and talk to Marapi."

"Will that do any good?" asked Peter.

"Probably not, but what else are you going to do?"

Peter studied the wall. The trees were all set firmly into the ground and tied together with thick ropes. They looked immovable, but if the ropes broke on a section and someone pushed really hard, it might be enough to topple them. An idea started to form. With a bit of luck they could do this without anyone getting hurt, he thought. Without anyone getting hurt much.

"Marapi accused Cerro of putting the village in danger," he said. "But she's taken Cassie prisoner, and she has no idea how dangerous that is. Rob, do you have a spare dagger?"

"I'm a pirate. Of course I've got a spare dagger."

"Good. Give it to Tom. We'll go through the wall. Tom, you'll need to run to the others and cut them free. Rob and

Bill will start fighting, which should gain you a little time. Stella, where is Marapi keeping your father?"

"There's only one hut with the door shut," she said. "Look, Peter, I know you mean well, but really you should let me talk to my aunt."

"What, so she can accuse you of helping pirates and lock you up with your father?" A nervous laugh rose in Peter's chest. He'd wanted to find out what he could do, and it turned out that what he did best was magic. Besides, they had Brine in there, and she'd always come for him when he'd needed help.

"Give me a few seconds," he said. "Come after me when you hear people screaming."

"Why are people going to scream?" asked Stella.

Peter put his hand in his pocket. "What does your biggest, scariest dinosaur look like?"

>++++++≥

It had been months since he'd used magic. Peter had spent all that time trying to not even think about it. Now, as he held the starshell piece, magic leaped into his hand as if it had always belonged there. Four quick bursts of light, and the ropes holding a section of wall flapped free. Then he took a deep breath and cast the disguise spell.

Marfak West had taught him how to do it a long time ago. You didn't draw a spellshape; instead you pictured the thing you wanted to be and you put the image on, like putting on a coat. Thinking of a bigger creature helped, he found, because the details were less fiddly. He pictured an animal like Boswell but minus the wings and with extra spines growing out of its back, and teeth that could bite through a tree. A disguisosaurus, he thought. He heard Stella cry out in surprise as he drew magic out of the starshell, but he didn't allow himself to react.

Focus.

The magic inflated the image around him. Peter stepped inside it, then braced himself and drew a downward arrow in the air. *Push.*

The wall gave way in front of him and he ran straight through. The nearest people screamed and scattered when they saw the disguisosaurus. Peter rushed at them. A spear sailed high over his head—of course, they weren't aiming at him: They were aiming at an imaginary dinosaur twenty times taller than him. He kept the disguise spell around him like a cloak and aimed another push spell at a hut, demolishing half of it with one blow.

Tom ran past, knife in hand. Bill and Rob were just behind. Stella followed them, an arrow fitted ready to her bow. A group of villagers charged at Tom with spears, but Peter lowered the disguisosaurus's head and made it roar at them, sending them fleeing. After all the months of holding back, it felt good. He thought of all the times his old master, Tallis Magus, had called him names, all the times Marfak

West had laughed at him, every time people had expected the worst from him just because he could use magic, and he channeled all the frustration into the spell.

He was supposed to find Stella's father, he remembered. He looked around and saw a hut with the door closed and two men standing outside. They fled as he turned in their direction, and he hit the hut door with a blast of magic that turned it to splinters.

Then Peter heard a shout and saw that Cassie was free.

It had been a long time since he'd seen Cassie fight, and he watched in amazement. She was barefoot, her clothes torn and bloodied, and she raged through the village like a storm. When she grabbed the first villager and hurled him aside, Peter was sure he heard bones break.

Tom was sawing at Brine's ropes now. One of the villagers ran at him, but Ewan Hughes suddenly broke free and barreled into him, a knife in each hand. Trudi joined him a moment later, then the villagers closed in around them and Peter couldn't see Brine and Tom any longer.

At the same moment, his starshell ran out of magic, the disguisosaurus vanished around him, and he stood in full view.

People turned to stare. Peter raised a hand and waved awkwardly. "Um, hello."

A teradon screamed down at him. Peter threw himself flat, feeling its claws graze the back of his head. He rolled out of the way, looking for Brine, and saw her struggling with a tall one-eyed woman holding a cutlass.

"That's Marapi," Stella said, pulling Peter to his feet. "Come on."

But Cassie got there first. She shoved Brine aside and tore the cutlass from Marapi's hand. "You poisoned my crew!" she yelled. "You stole my weapons. You think your dinosaur monsters are dangerous? Try me on for size!"

Marapi stumbled back from her. Cassie pushed her over and kicked her, then grabbed her by the hair and smacked her head hard onto the ground.

Peter winced.

"There you go," said Rob, pausing beside him. "Never laugh in the face of Cassie." He looked around for someone else to fight.

Peter ran to Brine and helped her up.

"You used magic," she said. She blinked dizzily at him then hugged him hard. Peter's face burned, but before he could speak, a voice cut through the noise.

"Enough!"

The single shouted word silenced Cassie's yelling and the clash of weapons. Everyone paused.

Peter turned to look at the hut he'd partly demolished. A man hobbled out of it, supporting himself on crutches.

"Cerro!" cried Stella, and ran to him. He paused to smile at her and then limped across to Marapi.

"What are you doing?" he demanded. "Are you completely mad?"

Marapi picked herself up. Blood dripped from her nose

and from a cut on her forehead. Her gaze was murderous. "I am protecting the village. Something that you should have been doing."

"It's a bit hard to do anything when your own sister locks you away," snapped Cerro. "And you call this protecting?"

Peter suddenly became uncomfortably aware of the broken wall, the smashed huts, and the islanders still gripping weapons fearfully. No wonder Stella wouldn't look at him. He'd promised to help her, and instead they'd flattened her village.

"Stella told me about her brother," he said. "We can get him back. And, um, I'm sorry we attacked you."

"Are we supposed to trust the word of a foreign magus now?" said Marapi. "He's a child; what can he do?"

He could turn her into a worm for a start, Peter thought, and his stomach twisted queasily at the notion. Although his starshell was empty, he stuffed it back into his pocket quickly.

Brine squeezed his hand. "Peter's one of the good ones."

"Yes, not evil at all," added Tom.

Peter didn't know whether to hit them or hug them. He compromised with an awkward flap of his arms. "Brine, this is Stella. Her brother's a prisoner in Orion's Keep, and we're going to rescue him."

Marapi's face turned even more thunderous, but Cassie smiled and put her cutlass away. "Someone needs rescuing? Why didn't you say so?"

"Because they were too busy tying us up and accusing us of spying." Trudi glowered.

"Oh yes, that." Cassie turned to Cerro. "I'm sure it was all a misunderstanding and we can sit down and sort everything out together." She kept smiling, but her eyes were narrowed and she never moved her hand far from her cutlass hilt.

Cerro shifted his grip on his crutches and held out his hand. "Cerro Erebus, and whatever my sister told you, I am the leader of Apcaron Island."

"Cassie O'Pia," said Cassie. "Captain of the pirate ship *Onion*."

A pause. A dark-brown hand met a light-brown one.

"What happened to Cassie's feet?" Peter whispered to Brine. Now that the fight was over, his head was starting to ache and he wanted to sit down.

"A dinosaur happened. I'll tell you about it later."

"Well done, Peter," said Ewan. He shoved his daggers through his belt. "Lucky I keep a pair of these down my trousers for emergencies."

"You keep daggers in your trousers?" said Peter. "Doesn't that hurt?"

He winked at them. "Only when I sit down."

CHAPTER 13

She's clearly not gutless when it comes to a cutlass;
She is skilled with her left hand and right.
If her fortunes reverse, well, things could be worse,
And she never turns tail from a fight.

(from THE BALLAD OF CASSIE O'PIA,
Verse 315, Author Unknown)

B rine's thoughts sang. Peter and Tom had come for her. Just as she knew they would and exactly at the right moment, just when Marapi was saying it would never happen. The whole thing had felt almost magical. Ewan Hughes was humming, and Brine bet he was making up more verses for the *Ballad of Cassie O'Pia*.

"This is madness," shouted Marapi. "These people attacked us—they destroyed our home—and now you're treating them like guests!"

Ewan Hughes broke off his humming. "Does anything rhyme with dinosaur?"

Marapi stared at him.

"How about Apcaron, then?" he asked cheerfully. "No? What is this, the land that rhyme forgot?"

Marapi opened and shut her mouth a few times, her single-eyed gaze filling up with venom. Brine grinned. Marapi liked to threaten everyone, she thought, but she didn't know what to do if people stood up to her.

Cerro started toward one of the huts. "Marapi, you are no longer in control here. You may come and sit quietly, or you can be tied up in a corner—it's your choice. Someone bring food. Bandages, too," he added, glancing at Cassie's feet.

A few of the villagers looked like they were going to argue, and then they caught Ewan's gaze and suddenly became very interested in nearby trees and rocks. Marapi still had support here, Brine thought: They'd have to be careful of that. She hung back from the main group and gazed from face to face, trying to find someone she recognized. There was no one. Her initial excitement after the fight slowly soured to disappointment. But what had she been hoping for exactly? That she'd take two steps onto the island and her parents would magically appear and shower her with dragons?

"Do you remember me?" she asked Stella.

Stella turned to stare at her. "Why would I remember you?"

"Because I might have lived here." Brine tried to push through the crowd after Cassie, but there were too many people and they wouldn't move, not even when she kicked them. "I was found on the other side of the world, and I can't remember how I got there. I must have come from some-where."

Stella peered at her closely then sighed and shook her head. "I'm sorry. But the magi started taking more kids to Orion's Keep two or three years ago—usually people whose parents had died. You might be one of those."

So her parents might be dead. Brine's hope curled up and died.

Peter and Tom squeezed back to join her. "They're talking," said Tom, adjusting his glasses, which had been knocked sideways in the crush. "It looks like it might go on a while."

Brine groaned and sat down on the grass. She wished she were back on the *Onion*, or even in Orion's Keep in the sky—anyplace other than this village where she clearly didn't be-long. And she missed Boswell. "We should be out looking for dragons, not sitting about here," she said. "Are there dragons in the flying castle?"

Stella snorted. "What is it with you people and dragons? No. There are no dragons in the castle. Or on the island. The castle is named after a dragon, if that helps—Orion's Keep."

Orion was a dragon? Brine wondered.

Tom was also shaking his head. "Orion's a sailor. He sailed his ship all the way north, into the sky."

"Orion is a dragon," said Stella firmly. "A lady dragon. According to the story, she lived on this island before there were any people. There was another dragon, Marfak, and he and Orion fought every day. In the end, Orion won and flew up into the stars, and Marfak was buried and became a volcano. That's why the volcano is called Marfak's Peak." She finally seemed to notice they were all staring at her. "What's wrong?"

"Marfak West named himself after a defeated dragon?" asked Tom. "That doesn't sound like him."

Brine hushed him. Her arms prickled with cold. She knew this story, she thought: Two dragons fighting—their golden bodies were like a bright flash of memory. She rubbed her hands over her face. "There's more, isn't there? Something about Orion returning?"

Stella gave her an odd look. "Orion's supposed to come back from the stars one day, and Marfak will burst out of the ground to fight her. Either that or Marfak will break free and Orion will return to fight him. In any case, the whole island will be destroyed. Cerro says it's just a warning about the volcano."

A vengeful, defeated enemy who was going to destroy everything. That sounded more like Marfak West.

"It's only a story," said Stella.

"There's no such thing as 'only a story.'" Brine picked a handful of grass and separated the stalks. "Every story starts with a little bit of truth. Sometimes it's not the truth you were expecting, but it's always there if you look for it." She scattered the last pieces of grass. She'd remembered a story—or she'd almost remembered it, which was just as good. At last, a piece of memory had come back. All she had to do now was find more pieces to fit around it.

"You said you tried to rescue your brother," she said. "How did you get into the castle?"

Stella hesitated. Then, as if she'd decided they might be able to help after all, she grinned. "I'll show you. It's just outside the village."

Brine looked back at the crowded hut and the four posts with ropes dangling off them like snakes. Marapi might be afraid of Cassie for now, but the village could turn unfriendly again very quickly. If Stella's brother needed rescuing, they should do it soon.

Tom hung back, but Brine dragged him after her. "I'm the chief planner, remember? Come on—you can blame me if this goes wrong."

It was a bag. Peter walked around it slowly. A bag big enough to hold a dinosaur, draped over bushes, tethered down at intervals, and attached with ropes to a basket woven out of thick green strands. It lay across fallen trees and undergrowth, striped golden with the afternoon sunlight.

"This is how you got to the castle? What did you do—catapult yourself in it?"

Stella lifted one edge of the fabric. "No, it's a balloon—Cerro invented it. He thought it would be a safe way of traveling around the island. You heat the air up inside the sack, and it lifts off the ground. It's just like flying."

That was impossible—you couldn't fly without magic. Peter hadn't even worked out how to do it *with* magic.

Something roared not too far away, and he jumped.

"We're safe here," said Stella. "Apart from the teradons, this area is dinosaur-free."

"Do the dinosaurs know that?" Peter poked at the balloon. "You must be using magic."

"It could work without," said Tom. "Hot air is lighter than cold. How do you heat the air? You light a fire underneath the balloon, I suppose."

"Actually," Stella said, "we do use magic for that part. We have heatstones. We use them for lighting fires normally, but if you put them in the mouth of the balloon, they'll heat the air. You just have to keep them away from the balloon fabric or it'll catch fire. The basket is made from dried sandvines—they're useful when they're dead. I was hunting some earlier when I found you."

"I have starshell," said Peter. He took it out and showed it to her. "I can make heat. And I'm good at pushing and pulling things." It had sounded impressive in his head. Out loud, it just sounded like he was trying to show off.

Stella picked the starshell out of his hand, looked at it for a moment, then shrugged. "It's a decently large piece. Not much use at the moment, though, is it?" She handed it back.

Peter had never met anyone who'd not been impressed by

magic before—he wasn't sure how to react. He put the starshell piece back in his pocket. "So you tried to rescue your brother. What happened?"

Stella's gaze clouded. "Cerro got into the castle, but when he found Ren, Ren didn't recognize him. He started shouting, and the guards came before Cerro could escape."

"Your brother didn't recognize his own father?" Peter interrupted sharply.

"Just like I've forgotten my parents," said Brine, sitting down on the ground.

Stella walked around the balloon. "Anyway," she said, "Cerro jumped off the castle to escape. He landed on the balloon, but he broke his legs in the fall, and I made things worse by crashing. Since then, I've been coming here every day since and making repairs."

She glared at them all defiantly. Cerro couldn't walk, and from what Stella had said, no one on the island was willing to help her. And yet, she hadn't given up.

"We'll get your brother back," said Peter. He wasn't sure how—the thought of flying beneath a bag of air made him feel queasy—but they'd do it.

Brine elbowed him in the side. "Peter isn't the one making the plan—I am—and my plans always work. Your mistake was going in secretly. You should never sneak in somewhere you can't escape from." She sketched a castle in the dirt with her finger. "We'll take as many people as we can fit in the basket and we'll fight."

Stella stopped walking. "Is she serious?"

Peter felt a grin break out. "Oh yes, completely serious." Brine was planning again.

"Let's see what Cassie says," Tom hedged.

But Peter already knew what Cassie would say. A magic castle, a stolen boy, and stories about dragons. Whole herds of dinosaurs couldn't keep her away.

CHAPTER 14

In the time of dragons, two dragons were greater than all the others, and their names were Orion and Marfak. Day and night they fought until Orion finally threw Marfak down into the earth, and a mountain sprang up to cover him. And Orion, in her triumph, flew up into the sky where her stars may still shine.

(APCARON LEGEND)

No," said Cassie.

She sat inside the hut, her legs stretched out, one of her feet bandaged. Ewan hunkered down next to her, two daggers stuck into the ground in front of him where he could reach them. Rob, Bill, and Trudi were all eating—plates of orange-red stew that smelled vaguely of apple.

Trudi held out her plate. "It's flying tree frog," she said. "Try it—it's better than it sounds."

It sounded completely horrible. Brine shook her head, her gaze still on Cassie. Brine must have misheard her; Cassie never turned down an adventure. She didn't dare look at Cerro, though she could feel him watching her, and Marapi, too.

"You can all stop looking at me like that," snapped Cassie. "I'm a pirate, not a bird. I am not flying."

"The balloon is perfectly safe," said Tom. "Well, in theory. How did you think we were going to get into the castle?"

Cassie shrugged. "I don't know. I thought there might be a secret tunnel or something."

"To a castle in the sky?"

"A secret tunnel makes more sense than a giant flying bag."

Cassie stood, balancing her weight on her left leg. "It's getting late. We'll return to the *Onion* for the night and make plans tomorrow."

"That's not fair," said Peter. "We promised."

"*You* promised," said Cassie. "I didn't. And you're already in enough trouble for wandering off without permission. We'll talk about this later. Right now we need to get back to the ship."

Cerro struggled to stand, but Marapi was faster, on her feet in an instant. "Didn't I say this would happen?" She jabbed a finger at Cassie. "Outsiders. Thieves and killers. You can't trust anything they say."

A mutter of agreement spread around them. Cassie dropped a hand to her cutlass. Another minute and they'd be fighting again, Brine thought. She pushed between Cassie and Marapi, hoping neither would draw a weapon at this particular moment.

"We'll come back tomorrow," she said. "The castle isn't

going anywhere. The magi can spend the night dreading our arrival if they like." She smiled, but her voice wobbled. Standing this close to Cassie, she could see how ill the pirate captain looked. Her eyes were ringed with shadow, and her face tightened with pain as she shifted her weight from foot to foot. Cassie never turned down a rescue, and she always kept going, no matter what. To see her looking pale and tired felt like part of the world had collapsed.

"I'll go with them on their ship," said Stella. "They'll need help avoiding the dinosaurs."

"No," said Cerro.

Marapi smiled and stepped back. "Very well," she said. "We'll let you go—but on one condition. Tomorrow, you will go to Orion's Keep and bring back my nephew. If you fail, then my brother's faith in you is unfounded and his judgment is unbalanced. He proves himself unfit to rule and he steps down."

Marapi didn't believe they'd come back, Brine thought. She was sending Stella off with the pirates so that she could take back control of the village. If Brine had still had her sword, she'd have pulled it out and hit her.

"And if they succeed, I prove myself entirely fit to rule," said Cerro. "And you stop interfering."

Marapi's single eye glittered with a mixture of malice and triumph. "Agreed. Shall we say sunset tomorrow?"

Cassie nodded curtly. "Sunset." She swayed and righted herself quickly, then let go of Ewan and limped away.

Brine swallowed a hard lump in her throat. "Don't worry," she told Stella. "Cassie never fails."

"She better not," replied the girl. "When this is over, you can get in your ship and sail away. I have to carry on living here."

🐟

Brine had never been so happy to see the *Onion*. She'd half expected to find the ship had vanished after everything else that had gone wrong that day, but the ship was exactly where they'd left her, floating, safe and familiar.

A small dragon-shaped missile catapulted into Peter's knees.

"He's missed you," said Tim Burre. "Where have you been?"

Brine wasn't sure where to start, but it didn't matter because Trudi and Rob launched into stories of dinosaurs, sinksand, and sandvines.

Boswell wriggled up over Peter's shoulder, setting fire to the back of his shirt. Brine patted out the flames quickly.

"That's a dragon," said Stella.

Brine grinned, enjoying the mix of confusion and outrage on the older girl's face. She remembered the feeling of finding out the world was a lot bigger than you'd imagined. "Dragons?" she said innocently. "They're just stories."

Peter shifted his grip on Boswell so he could scratch the dragon's belly. "I'll show you around," he said to Stella. "Coming, Brine?"

But Brine shook her head. "I'll stay here for a while."

She sat at the edge of the deck, watching as the last of the daylight faded and the island was swallowed by darkness.

Her thoughts buzzed like insects in annoying circles. So far, Dragon Island had completely failed to be anything like she'd expected. No dragons, and she was no closer to finding her family.

Cassie's voice drifted out. "Ewan, take charge. I'm going to bed. Wake me if anything happens."

They should all get some sleep, Brine thought, but she wasn't tired. The magicians at Orion's Keep must know they were here. What were they waiting for?

She looked up as Tom sat beside her. "You'd think I would remember something," she said. "This is all going wrong."

"It'll be fine," said Tom. "We can rest tonight, and tomorrow you can make us a rescue plan." He pushed his glasses up and grinned. "Maybe Peter can work out the spellshape for magicking us up to the castle so we won't have to use the balloon."

"And maybe Peter will make a mistake and drop you all into the volcano by mistake," said Peter, strolling back across the deck with Stella and Boswell in tow. "When I decide to experiment with new spellshapes, I'll do it on my own. I don't want anyone getting hurt."

He smiled, but Brine knew he was serious. This wasn't just him not knowing the spellshape. Peter had used magic without spellshapes before. He was still worried about using magic.

Boswell pawed at Stella's leg, and she crouched to stroke him. "I can't believe you have a dragon. Did you really find him at the top of the world?" Her voice held a note of wistfulness. "It must be nice to live on a ship, to go anywhere you want."

"We like it," said Brine. "Of course, there's always the chance you'll drown in a storm or get eaten by sea-monsters."

"But you'd be free," said Stella. She sat back, tilting her head up to the stars. "I never told Cerro this, but when we were building the balloon, I thought that once we'd rescued Ren, I might go flying, just for the fun of it. To see what else is out there."

Brine smiled, looking down at the deck. She'd come here wanting to find her home and she'd met a girl who wanted to fly away and see the world. "We could ask Cassie . . . ," she began.

Boswell bolted upright, and Stella yelled in pain as his claws went into her legs. "What's he doing?" She tried to lift him up, but he clung to her, hissing at first, and then he began to howl.

An answering howl came from the sky. Brine sat up straight. More dragons? But there weren't any dragons— Stella had said so.

Dark wings cut across the sky—lots and lots of them.

"Teradons," said Stella, and then it was raining yellow streaks.

The streaks landed in sizzling blotches all over the deck.

One of them landed on Brine and she yelled, partly because it stung, but mostly because of the smell, which was like rotten eggs mixed with bananas and the very worst of Trudi's curry.

"They're bombarding us," said Tom. A yellow streak landed on his glasses. "I've seen seagulls do this to drive off enemies. I wonder if teradons are related to seagulls."

Brine didn't really care either way. She tore Boswell from Stella's legs and ran for the hatch to belowdecks, the howling dragon in her arms. More disgusting-smelling streaks landed around her. An extra-large patch had half a dead rat in it. At least, Brine thought it was a rat; she didn't really stop to look.

"Raise the anchor!" shouted Ewan. "They're probably just protecting their territory. We'll let them think we're running away, and . . . and, someone, get me a towel."

The *Onion* began to move. Ewan scrubbed dinosaur droppings off his arms. Boswell stopped howling and started clawing at Brine, trying to get free. Brine pulled him back. "You can't fight them, you silly dragon."

Boswell turned his head and blew hot air into her face. Brine let him go in surprise and, instead of falling, he spread his wings and glided, landing out of reach.

Tom laughed with amazement. "He's trying to fly!"

A teradon screamed down out of the sky at them. Brine yelled and ducked, but Boswell began flapping his wings and rose unsteadily off the deck to meet it.

Brine's heart leaped into her throat. The teradon was

twenty times the size of Boswell. As the teradon wheeled aside, Boswell flapped backward, his wings beating unevenly. Then, gaining his balance, he took off in pursuit. The sky darkened with wings then lit with bright flashes of dragon fire.

The teradons retreated—all of them. Brine gazed into the sky, her mouth open in amazement, until another yellow blob landed nearby, and she snapped it shut. A few more streaks spattered down. Teradons shouted overhead, their cries growing more distant, and their cries were echoed by a half roar, half meow that sounded so furious, nobody on board the ship dared laugh.

Boswell circled the ship twice, then landed back in the middle of the deck and folded his wings.

Everyone stumbled back onto the deck, trying to skirt the smelly patches.

"They all just *fled*," said Stella, incredulous. "Teradons aren't afraid of anything. And Boswell's only a baby."

Tom scratched his head with a pen. "Once, on Barnard's Reach, we had a really bad winter, and a pair of storm eagle chicks took shelter on the cliffs. The other birds had never seen a storm eagle before, and yet every bird flew up in a panic. It was like something inside them knew what an eagle was, and knew to stay away."

"You're saying that dinosaurs instinctively recognize dragons and run away from them?" asked Brine.

Tom's pen was tangled in his hair. "Do you have any better ideas?" he asked, tugging at his head.

"Not really."

Peter held a hand out to Boswell, and the dragon trotted to him. "If dinosaurs recognize dragons, it must be that at some point in the past, dinosaurs have seen dragons." His face flushed with excitement.

"So there might have been dragons here once," said Brine cautiously. This island had already disappointed her. She didn't want Peter disappointed, too.

"Why is my ship covered in yellow?" asked Cassie, limping out onto the deck.

Brine gave a silent cheer to see her. Bill Lightning started explaining how they were attacked by monstrous flying beasts the size of the ship and Boswell had fought them all off.

"He deserves extra supper tonight," said Brine. "I'll go and see what Trudi's got. Are you coming?" She included Stella in the invitation, and the girl nodded eagerly. Peter, though, shook his head.

"I'm going to keep watch, just in case those things come back."

He wanted to be on his own again, he meant. Brine wished he didn't, but trying to persuade him out of it would only make him grumpy.

CHAPTER 15

DRAGON ISLAND SUPPER

3 sandvines, chopped (watch out for the thorns)

1 strange brown mammal with a long nose

2 handfuls of various colored mushrooms

Many handfuls of assorted green leaves, plants, and vines,
    all guaranteed nonpoisonous. Probably.

Boil together. The flavors were strange, especially the sea-
    weed, but nobody has died yet—so it's probably safe.

(from COOKING UP A STORME—
THE RECIPES OF A GOURMET PIRATE)

Peter waited until Brine and Tom were in the galley and fussing over Boswell before he crept down the length of the ship to the darkest space at the back and squeezed in between the crates.

It wasn't long before Marfak West appeared.

"Hiding again?" asked the ghost.

Peter gave him a blank stare. "You know I'm not. I'm having a break. I think I deserve one after everything that's happened. We heard the story about Orion and

Marfak, by the way. Why did you name yourself after a dead volcano?"

The ghost studied his fingernails. "The volcano isn't dead; it's dormant. One day it will erupt, and then the whole island will pay for not taking the threat seriously."

Peter understood. If there was one thing Marfak West hated, it was people not taking him seriously. "What was your name before you changed it to Marfak West?" he asked curiously.

The ghost flickered irritably. "That's completely irrelevant."

Peter grinned. "Why? Was it something really stupid, like Fish-Face or Slimehead?"

"For your information," said the ghost, drawing himself up, "it was Borage."

Peter struggled to keep a straight face. "Borage? Seriously?"

"It's an herb—with purple flowers, apparently. My mother liked gardening and purple. If I'd been a girl, I would have been called Lavender. And if you breathe a word of this to anyone, that will be the last time you ever breathe."

Borage the Evil Magician didn't sound half as impressive as Marfak West. Peter grinned again, still trying to get his mind around the idea of Marfak West having a mother. He must have had one, of course, but people like Marfak West and Cassie seemed to appear in the world fully formed, and it felt odd to think of them growing up. "Not a word," Peter promised. He actually quite liked the idea of sharing a secret with the magician. "How about doing something for me in return? How do we get into the flying castle? Is there a spellshape for it?"

Marfak West shrugged. "I expect so. But it's been a long time since I've used it, and my memory isn't what it used to be. I might be able to remember it—if you do something for me."

"What's that?" asked Peter.

"Kill Cassie O'Pia."

Peter almost choked on his laughter. "Not a chance."

"Then enjoy your balloon trip," said the ghost, and he faded away into the air.

><+++}}+o

P eter squeezed out between the crates and made his way through the ship. He could hear Brine, Tom, and Stella talking in the galley.

"But what's it *for*?" Stella asked.

"Well, he's furry," Brine said, "which is nice when the weather is cold. His whiskers are tickly. And he caught a rat once—or so Cassie said. He prefers fish."

Peter crept on past. All the hammocks were occupied, so he climbed back up to the deck.

How had Marfak West known about the balloon? Had he been spying on them? Peter shuddered. Shaking his head, he climbed out onto the deck. Rob and Bill were sitting in a circle of pirates, trying to outdo each other with stories about sinksand and teradons.

"With claws as long as your arm," said Bill. "And teeth so sharp, they can bite the air in two."

Then Peter saw Cassie. She was sitting at the edge of the deck, gazing down at the sea. She didn't turn around when Peter approached, though she must have heard his footsteps.

"How's the leg?" asked Peter.

"I won't have to replace it with a wooden one just yet." She flashed him a smile. "Are you sure you can't magic us up to the castle? There must be a spellshape."

Yes, and he'd have to kill her to get it. "I don't know," said Peter. His stomach felt like he'd swallowed a bag of snakes, all of them writhing poisonously inside him. He clutched the starshell piece in his pocket so tightly, the edge bit into his hand. "Tom thinks the balloon will work, and he knows about these things. And I can use magic if anything goes wrong. Probably."

"You want us to fly to a magic castle using a large bag of hot air. What could possibly go wrong?" Cassie moved over for him to sit down, and went back to staring at the sea.

He only had himself to blame, Peter thought, sitting next to her. If he'd spent the past months experimenting with magic instead of hiding from it, he might be able to work out the spellshape for himself—or do it without a spellshape. He knew he could, after all—Marfak West had taught him that.

Cassie looked up, meeting Peter's gaze. "Do you want to know a secret?"

"What?"

"I'm afraid of heights."

Peter shook his head and laughed. Cassie wasn't afraid of anything.

"It's true," she said. She twisted the emerald around her neck. "Did Brine ever tell you how I ran away from home after my brother put me up as a prize in a fight?"

According to most of the stories, it was Cassie's father and he'd lost her in a game of cards. Brine had never said anything to Peter about it. He shook his head.

"Well, anyway, the story isn't quite true," said Cassie. "It's not a complete lie, either—dig deep enough, and you'll find a scrap of truth in any story. The truth is, my brother was a bully. He enjoyed scaring me. One of his favorite games was to hold me out of the upstairs window. Sometimes he'd drop me. We had thick bushes underneath, so I was never badly hurt, but it used to terrify me. No one ever stopped him or punished him for it because he was a boy and the oldest. I was supposed to put up with it."

Her hands dropped to her lap. "One day I stopped putting up with it. I still don't know why. I think I'd just had enough of being frightened of him. So, as he tried to push me out of the window, I jammed my feet on either side on the wall and then grabbed hold of him and beat him half to death. I kicked him so hard, I broke a couple of toes, but it was completely worth it."

Peter gazed at her, openmouthed. He'd only ever known Cassie the pirate captain. He'd never thought of her being a child, being afraid and fighting back anyway.

"You can stop looking at me like that," said Cassie irritably.

"Like what?"

"Like I'm some sort of hero." She brushed her hand across her eyes. "I fought him because I was terrified of him. I didn't stop even when he was unconscious. In the end, I came to my senses and found I was holding him by the ears and banging his head into the wall, over and over. That finally made me stop. And then what do you think I did?"

Peter didn't know what to say. He shrugged, imagining various possibilities, none of them good.

"Nothing," said Cassie. "I was terrified all over again—scared of what my brother would do when he woke, what my parents would do when they found out. So I ran away. I stowed away on a boat and then talked the captain into letting me stay. I spent a couple of years moving from ship to ship until I ended up on the *Onion*." She lifted the emerald around her neck. "This belonged to my mother—the only thing she had that was worth anything. I stole it when I ran away. I meant it to be a reminder of home, but it didn't turn out that way. It's a warning of who I can be if I'm not careful—a coward, lashing out in fear."

"It wasn't your fault," said Peter.

"Wasn't it? I beat him senseless and I enjoyed it. For all I know, I killed him that day—I've never been back to find out. That's how brave I am."

Peter swallowed the lump in his throat. He'd always been jealous of Brine, he thought, her closeness with Cassie, the way Cassie told her things she never told anyone else. He got the feeling this was something she'd never even shared with Brine, and Peter knew he would never tell Brine about it.

Cassie went back to staring at the sea.

"Marfak West made me turn the Mother Keeper of Barnard's Reach into a worm," said Peter.

"I know. I saw her afterward. That wasn't you—Marfak West was using you."

"Yes, but . . ." He paused and swallowed. "But, looking back on it, I sort of enjoyed it. Being able to do something like that. And I'd tried to warn her that Marfak West was back and Barnard's Reach was in danger, but she just kept going on about the rules and it was really annoying. I think that's why I couldn't turn her back afterward: because some part of me thought she deserved to be a worm."

He'd never told anyone this, not even Brine, certainly not Tom, whose mother was the new Mother Keeper of the library island. Peter had never even allowed himself to think about it in any detail. Saying the words out loud made him feel like something nasty was coming out of him. He felt a bit ill, but also better in some strange way, as if the snakes were still there in his stomach but were all settling down to sleep.

Cassie gave a ghost of a smile. "You are not Marfak West."

"How do you know?" asked Peter. "Marfak West used to be a normal person, and then magic corrupted him. What if the same thing happens to me? What if I turn evil and you have to kill me?"

Cassie stood up and offered him her hand. "You have something Marfak West never did: We'll knock you over the head long before you become so evil that we have to kill you."

"Thanks," Peter said. He took Cassie's hand and got up. The clouds shifted, and for a moment he could see the constellation of Orion shining bright above them. A victorious dragon, he thought, or a mariner, showing the way to all ships on the eight oceans.

"Is there really no other way to the castle?" asked Cassie.

"Not that I know of."

She nodded. "And if I don't rescue Stella's brother, none of you will ever speak to me again."

"Oh, we'll speak to you," said Peter. "Though maybe not for a while." He flashed her a smile. "This isn't only about Stella's brother, though. There are three magicians in the castle, and if anyone knows what happened to the dragons here, they will. It might be another dead end, but we have to try."

Cassie laughed.

"What?" asked Peter.

"Nothing. I was just thinking how you hardly ever get dead ends at sea." She grasped his shoulder. "You're right: We should try. Let's get some sleep now, and tomorrow we'll go and face our fears."

CHAPTER 16

She fought dinosaurs on mysterious shores,
To all fear she's completely immune.
Like Orion, she flew, rising into the blue,
And conquered a castle by balloon.

(from THE BALLAD OF CASSIE O'PIA,
Verse 222, Author Unknown)

It felt like ages until Cassie came out on deck the next morning. Brine spent the time pacing.

"Can't you sit down?" Peter asked her.

She paused, but anytime she stood still, it felt like her insides were being eaten by fire ants. She didn't know how Peter could stay so calm. Tom and Stella, too. They were all sitting, the remains of breakfast spread around them as if this were any ordinary day.

"Don't you want to rescue Stella's brother?" asked Brine.

Peter waved a frog kebab at her. "Of course. But . . ."

The only "but" that Brine could think of was that they'd had to leave Boswell locked in the galley because they couldn't risk him flying after them. Although if Cassie didn't hurry up, it wouldn't make any difference, because Boswell was going to claw his way right through the door.

Finally, Cassie appeared, wearing a plain dark shirt and trousers with a cutlass on one hip and a long dagger on the other. She didn't look like someone trying to make an impression today; she looked like she meant business. She strode across deck with no hint of a limp.

"So," she said, "who wants to get in a basket under a bag of air and fly to a magic castle to rescue the son of a stranger?"

Brine laughed weakly, but she was the only one.

This was a crazy, guaranteed-to-get-them-all-probably-killed plan—in other words, the sort of thing Cassie liked best, but Cassie had the look of someone who was about to walk the plank, and she wasn't the only one. Ewan Hughes's face was grim, and Trudi chewed her hair nervously. Tom darted away and came back clutching large, empty sacks. Peter gripped his box of starshell pieces in both hands, his face a seasick green.

Cassie clapped her hands. "Right. I'm going in the balloon, of course. Ewan, Rob, Bill, Trudi, and Peter, too. And Stella will have to fly the thing. She'll take us to the castle and then we'll defeat the magicians and make them tell Peter the spellshape for getting back to the ground. Brine and Tom, you're in charge here. If anything goes wrong, Stella will need your help."

Brine and Tom shouted together.

Cassie sighed heavily. "I know you want to come, but it's too dangerous. We wouldn't take Peter, either, but we need his magic. No offense, Tom, but what are you going to do in a fight—write people to death?"

Tom shoved his hands into his pockets. "It's just as dangerous staying here. What if those teradons attack us again? Besides, you haven't heard my plan."

Brine turned to stare at him. "You have a plan?"

Tom took off his glasses and cleaned them on the edge of his sack. "You're not the only one with plans, you know. We're flying a balloon to a castle full of evil magicians. I think they might notice. We can't just sneak in and rescue people—we need a distraction. A better distraction than waving your cutlasses about," he added quickly as Ewan grinned.

"Waving cutlasses about is the definition of a distraction," replied Ewan.

"If you want to get killed or captured very quickly, yes. But if you'd like to try something that might actually work, I have an idea. The castle is full of magic, right? It's the only way it can possibly stay up. And we know what happened to the sea-spiders when they ate a load of magic-filled ship."

Ewan raised an eyebrow. "And?"

Tom waved the sack at him. "And I was wondering, can we get hold of any sandvines?"

They skirted around the village and made their way to the balloon. Brine jumped at every sound, convinced that another dinosaur was going to come stampeding through the trees, but Stella didn't seem worried.

"They usually stay closer to the river," she said. "And we've killed enough of them that they don't tend to go after big groups of people."

Brine wasn't convinced, but she kept walking, and they arrived at the balloon with no sign of ferocious beasts.

Ewan gave the basket a kick and glared at it, as if daring it to fall apart. He looked almost disappointed when it didn't.

"This isn't natural," moaned Cassie, climbing in. "People should not fly around in the sky like birds."

"I bet there was a time when people said ships were unnatural," said Tom. "One day, flying will take the place of sailing."

Cassie covered her eyes. "I hope not."

━┤┤╫●

The basket creaked under the weight of the pirates and sacks of sandvines. Stella produced a handful of starshell fragments. "Heatstones," she said, rubbing them between her hands. She set them in a metal dish beneath the balloon, and the fabric began to ripple and swell with air.

"Ready?" asked Stella after a minute or two. She cut the ropes anchoring them to the ground, and they shot into the sky. Brine's insides were almost left behind in the rush. She tried to stay standing, but her legs had other ideas and she curled up on the basket floor. They were all mad, she thought: mad as a hot winter.

The one good thing was that the magicians in the castle would never expect a fish-brained scheme like this.

The balloon rose higher and higher.

"If I pass out," Cassie said to Ewan, "promise to catch me."

Ewan grinned. "I won't let you go. Don't worry. This could be worse."

Cassie buried her face in her knees with another groan.

"Though not much," admitted Ewan.

As if to prove him wrong, something on the castle battlements let out an earsplitting shriek. Brine clapped her hands over her ears, but the noise still made her head spin.

"Guardgoyles!" Stella shouted. "We're almost there." She dropped a pair of ropes over the side of the basket. "I'll take you over the castle, and then you'll need to climb down. Don't worry. It'll be fine."

"What do you mean, fine?" Brine shouted back. "It's the opposite of fine. It's so far away from being fine that—"

Ewan disappeared over the side of the basket.

"Go!" cried Stella.

Rob and Bill jumped after him, then Cassie bellowed and flung herself over as well. Brine saw them all sliding down the ropes. Her vision blurred dizzily. It was only a rope, she told herself. She'd climbed down ropes before. She closed her eyes, and, trying to pretend she was safely on board the *Onion*, she swung out into the sky.

It felt like she hung there forever, and then her feet touched solid stone. The guardgoyles stopped howling at once. The sudden silence left Brine's ears ringing, then a door slammed open and guards ran through. Ewan tackled the first one. Cassie drew her cutlass, but she looked unsteady.

"Look out," said Tom, and threw a handful of sandvines. They writhed on the stone floor as they stretched their roots into the stone and began to grow.

It got a bit confusing then, with people running and shouting and fighting while vines shot up everywhere and grabbed anyone within reach. The sandvines had no idea of friend or enemy and simply went for everybody. One of them wrapped around a guard and jerked him off his feet. Another attacked Bill, and more grew up around Ewan and Cassie as they fought. Cassie's cutlass flashed faster and faster, alternately attacking guards and fending off vegetation.

Tom threw another sandvine.

Brine spotted a door on the corner tower and grabbed Peter. "Come on."

The door opened before they reached it, and Brine skidded to a halt, gripping Peter's arm. Three people emerged—two men and a woman.

Brine knew straightaway by their robes and the gold-banded staff each carried that these were the magicians. And if she had needed another clue, their staffs glowed.

Brine's allergy to magic had burned itself out at Magical North, but it suddenly felt like it was back. Her head throbbed and her nose ached with the need to sneeze. "Peter—" she said. In a blur, she saw Cassie and Ewan turn, and Tom started toward her. Peter opened his box full of starshell and Brine felt him trembling.

Then one of the magicians gave a hoarse cry. "Oshima?" he said.

His voice tore through Brine's thoughts. Sandvines swarmed around her feet, pirates and guards were fighting, but everything suddenly seemed terribly far away. A cold weight filled her chest, pulling her down until her knees buckled and she collapsed onto the castle stones. Memories came tumbling out, none of them quite making sense, but gradually fitting together.

No wonder the island hadn't felt like home. She hadn't come from the island; she'd come from the castle. The magi hadn't taken her; she'd belonged here all along.

Brine rubbed her hands over her face, her vision blurring. "Who are you?"

"You don't remember," said the magician. The light around his staff faded. "I am Belen Kaya," he said, and Peter raised his starshell. "First Magus of Orion's Keep." His voice broke. "And, I think . . ." He took several quick steps forward and then knelt down in front of Brine. "I think I might be your father."

CHAPTER 17

The castle is here to keep the island. To keep it safe from
harm, to keep everything in its current state. That is why it is
called Orion's Keep: Our purpose is to preserve. That is our
first rule.

(from THE HISTORY OF ORION'S KEEP)

P eter might as well have been caught in sinksand. He let
his hands fall to his sides while around him, everything
paused. Stella's balloon hung motionless overhead; on the
battlements, pirates and guards paused, their swords still
raised. Even the sandvines grew quiet. How could the man be
Brine's father? He must be lying, but she wasn't trying to get
away from him. She knelt, gazing at him, her hands gripped
in his, while tears made trails down her cheeks.

Belen Kaya climbed stiffly to his feet. He looked just as
shocked as Brine, but he was smiling broadly. "I always knew
you'd come home," he said softly. "Always hoped it—and here
you are."

Peter bent and gripped Brine's arm. "Is this true?"

"I don't know." She wiped her eyes. Her expression was dazed, disbelieving. "I think . . . I know him. I know this castle. Cassie, stop fighting!"

Cassie turned around, her cutlass still in her hand. "But we've only just started." She swayed and took a step forward, then her legs buckled and she collapsed.

"Cassie!" shouted Ewan. The pirates ran to her.

Cassie groaned but didn't open her eyes. Muttering angrily, Ewan sliced through her trouser leg and boot.

Peter gasped when he saw her leg—it was swollen to almost twice its proper size, puffed up around the bandages, and the bandages themselves were soaked in blood.

"She said she was fine," muttered Ewan.

Of course she had. Cassie's leg could be falling off and she'd say it could be worse.

Belen Kaya made his way across and knelt down beside her. "What happened to her?"

"A dinosaur bit her," said Brine. Peter could feel her shaking. He squeezed her hand. She didn't look at him, but she squeezed back. A moment ago this was all clear—the magi were the enemy and all he had to do was fight them and rescue the children imprisoned in the castle. But now Cassie was hurt, and one of the magi might be Brine's father. Peter looked at Tom for answers, but Tom only shrugged. He clearly didn't know what was happening, either.

"The infection has spread right through her leg," said the magus. "I'm surprised she was able to stand at all. You'd better bring her inside."

The pirates shifted uneasily. Ewan put his hand on his sword. "I'm not bringing her anywhere."

"Then she'll die." Belen Kaya's gaze shifted to Peter. "Unless you know some very complicated healing spells."

Peter's cheeks grew hot. "I don't know any healing spells at all."

"I thought not. Wild magic."

Peter didn't know what he meant by that. His throat felt hot and dry. Cassie couldn't die. Cassie survived everything—it was as certain as the sun rising in the morning, or a dinosaur biting your leg off given half a chance.

The magus rose to his feet. "This fight is over. Put your weapons away, bring your friend inside, and we'll talk."

Ewan glanced at Brine as if to see what she wanted to do, but Brine stared down at the castle stones, biting her lip. Peter answered for her. "Do as he says," he said. "We don't have any choice."

This wasn't how he'd imagined it ending. A heroic battle, a grand rescue—that was how it had all played out in his head. Not a scrappy little fight and an enemy who might not be an enemy at all. Peter looked out over the battlements and saw Stella's balloon sinking away in the direction of the village. There was no way to tell her what had happened, so all he could do was follow the others down into Orion's Keep.

Belen Kaya led the way down a flight of stone steps and they all crowded into a room with a wooden bed. The rugs on the floor were richly patterned with dark red and gold and must have been expensive when they were new, but that was a long time ago, Peter reckoned, noticing the worn patches. In fact, everything about the castle looked worn—the flowers painted on the ceiling were peeling away, and a silver bowl on the bedside table was scratched and tarnished.

Ewan put Cassie down onto the bed. "If anything happens to her, I will kill you," he said, wearing a hard, bright smile. "Just so you know."

The magus nodded. "And if you threaten the castle again, I will throw you off the battlements." He matched Ewan's smile. "Just so you know."

He meant it, too, Peter thought. He bumped his hand against Brine's, but she didn't look up. She hadn't spoken since they'd left the battlements.

"You may call me Kaya," the magus said, starting to unwrap the bandages on Cassie's leg. More blood welled up. Kaya motioned to the two younger magicians to help. "This is Hiri and Ebeko. They have been studying magic since they were children."

In other words, don't mess with them, Peter thought.

Hiri gave them a nervous smile. Ebeko kept up the same scowl she'd worn on the castle battlements.

"Where's everyone else?" asked Tom. "This castle is big enough for a hundred people."

Peter tried not to stare at Cassie's leg. "Where is everyone else?"

Kaya frowned. "There is no one else. We have a few guards and helpers, but we are the last of the magi. Now, I'm going to need quiet to concentrate on the healing spells. You may wait outside. Oshima, you may stay if you wish."

Peter wondered who he was talking to until Brine shook her head. Oshima, he remembered—Kaya's daughter. Was it true?

"I'll stick with Peter and Tom," said Brine, and Peter looked down to hide his smile. Brine might be Kaya's daughter, but she was their friend first.

Ewan Hughes leaned against the wall and folded his arms. The look on his face said what he'd do to anyone who tried to move him.

Trudi took hold of Rob and Bill. "Ewan will stay, and the rest of us will wait outside. You're keeping children here, aren't you? We'll go and see them while you're concentrating."

Peter had almost forgotten about the children. He thought Kaya would refuse, but Trudi stretched her smile even wider and stared at the old magus until even Peter started to feel uncomfortable.

Kaya sighed. "Whatever they told you on the island, we don't hurt children. If you want to see them, Ebeko will take you."

ix children—four boys and two girls—sat together in the middle of a room full of toys and books. The floor was covered in animal skins, which made the room seem warmer but also gave it a funny smell.

Peter walked in slowly, stepping around the rugs. Someone in the past, it appeared, had decided it was a good idea to paint colorful pictures of dinosaurs all around the walls, but the paint was flaking off, so they looked a bit disfigured. Shelves poked out of one wall, holding a collection of books and wooden animals.

After what Stella had said, Peter had been expecting a prison, but someone had clearly gone to a lot of trouble to make this place comfortable. The children didn't seem to mind, though. They sat quietly, not speaking, not even looking up when the pirates crowded into the room. If the sight of Trudi, Rob, and Bill together couldn't get a child's attention, something was very wrong, Peter thought.

"What have you done to them?" he asked.

"Nothing." Ebeko stopped in the doorway. "We brought them here to train as new magi. They were fine at the start, but then they started to become confused, forgetting things. And now it's as if they've forgotten the rest of the world exists. If you put food in front of them, they'll eat it, and if you tell them to do something, they'll do it. So we know they can still understand us. But apart from that, they just sit."

Losing their memories, just like Brine. Though she'd never been as bad as this, Peter thought. He waved his hands in front of one of the girls. She stared at him, blank-faced.

"We're taking good care of them," said Ebeko, "and we've been trying to find a cure. It's slow work, but Kaya says we're getting closer."

"Can't you just take them back to the village for now?" asked Tom.

Ebeko shook her head sharply. "No. That would be the worst thing. The villagers already don't like us. If they saw the children like this, they'd never let us near them again, and then we'd have no hope of curing them."

And also, if people knew what was happening, they'd never send any children to the castle again, Peter thought—there would be no new magicians.

But if they didn't take Stella's brother home by sunset, Marapi would be claiming victory. Peter looked around at the others. Tom was looking at the books and toys on the shelves. Brine paced back and forth across the rugs, her face set in a frown so deep it looked permanent.

"We could always fight you again," said Trudi.

"No," said Peter, standing up. They couldn't leave until Cassie woke, and it seemed that Ren and the other children were only part of the mystery here. Was Kaya really Brine's father? And why did Orion's Keep even exist? A castle floating magically over a mountain—it made no sense.

Brine stopped pacing. "If Kaya is my father, what about the rest of my family?"

"You'll have to talk to Kaya about that," Ebeko said, looking away.

"You must remember Brine, though?" said Tom. "If there are only a few people in the castle, you must have noticed when one of them went missing."

Ebeko scratched at her arm. "I remember Kaya's daughter, Oshima. Your friend here is about the right age. Excuse me a moment."

She left, letting the door swing shut behind her.

"I thought she was supposed to be guarding us," said Trudi.

Peter was quite glad to see the magician go; the way she kept glaring at him made him uncomfortable.

Brine sat down next to the children. "This should be me," she said faintly. "This *would* have been me if I hadn't ended up in the Atlas Ocean. Am I going to start forgetting again?"

"You'll be fine," said Trudi. "Anyway, we won't be here long. Just long enough to get Cassie back on her feet, and then we'll take the children to the village. It's a pity there aren't any dragons, but maybe we'll find some on the next island."

Brine sniffed.

Peter squeezed her shoulder. "It's the shock, that's all."

"Shock?" Brine rubbed her hands over her eyes. "Sailing off the edge of the world was a shock. The plant monster was a shock. Getting chased by dinosaurs was a shock. This is . . ."

She trailed off, shaking her head. "If he's my father, how did I end up on the other side of the world? Why can't I remember what happened?" The last words barely made it out. Her shoulders slumped. "I'm supposed to be good at plans. I wish I knew what to do."

Peter wished the same thing. They'd come here on a rescue mission, but it was suddenly all a lot more complicated. He felt like they'd found a page torn from a book, and they had to work out what the rest of the book was about, and whether they could trust any of it. The more they saw of this island, the less they seemed to know what was going on.

Tom sat down with them. "We'll think of something."

"In fact, we'll think of something now," said Peter. If Brine wasn't up to making plans, then they'd have to do it for her. He pulled Brine and Tom close, casting a glance at the pirates, who were poking at the dinosaurs on the walls. "You remember when we joined the *Onion*?" he whispered. "We knew the crew was hiding things from us. So we divided up the questions and talked to everyone, remember?"

Brine nodded. "I haven't started forgetting things yet. I also remember that it didn't work."

Peter grinned at her. The shock must be wearing off if Brine was snapping at him. "But we're better at it now, aren't we?" he said. "And there are three of us this time, so it'll be twice as easy."

"Um, not quite," said Brine, but she was beginning to smile. "What do you want us to do?"

"Talk to Kaya," said Peter. "Find out everything you can about this castle. Tom, you find out what you can about these children. Ebeko is hiding something. Cerro wouldn't have built a balloon and flown here unless he had a good reason."

Tom's head bobbed enthusiastically. "I'll start investigating. What are you going to do?"

Peter glanced back at Trudi, who was edging closer, pretending she wasn't trying to eavesdrop. He grinned. The world felt better now that they had something to do. "I'm going to look for dragons," he said.

The door opened and Ebeko came back in. Peter wondered whether she'd been using magic to listen to them, but he thought she'd be acting a bit more suspiciously if she had, and she didn't seem suspicious at all. Unless you counted the smile she gave them.

"Good news," she said. "Kaya is finished. Your friend is going to live."

CHAPTER 18

Aldebran Boswell says that no matter how far you travel in the world, you cannot get away from who you are. He's right. In fact, you often don't find out who you truly are until you travel. There is nothing like going on a grand adventure to find out what you're made of.

(from THOMAS GIRLING'S SECRET BOOK
OF PIRATING ADVENTURE)

Cassie lay motionless, her eyes closed and her sun-bronzed face ash-pale, so still that Brine couldn't be sure she was even breathing.

"Don't worry," said Kaya, "she's alive. She just needs to rest. I had to use one spell to remove the poisons from her body, another to repair the damage to her leg, and another to speed up her body's own healing. She'll sleep for the rest of the day, but she'll be back on her feet within a week."

"A week?" echoed Brine. She sat down on the edge of the bed. What were they supposed to do for a week? Her head throbbed with pain, her throat ached, and her nose felt completely blocked. She'd come home—she'd found her father. Supposedly. She ought to be celebrating, but instead she felt like crying.

Talk to Kaya. Find out everything she could.

"Did you find the child?" asked Ewan.

Brine rubbed a hand over her eyes. "Yes, but . . . I think it's best if he stays here for now. He's safe."

She knew what that meant—they wouldn't be taking Ren home by sunset. Cerro would be disgraced and Marapi would take the opportunity to seize control of the village again. Stella was going to hate them all.

But what else could they do? They couldn't leave Cassie here alone. Besides, they had to find out what was wrong with the children, and the answers lay here in Orion's Keep, not in the village.

Brine expected Ewan to argue. Maybe he would have if he weren't worried about Cassie. He frowned and then nodded. "All right, if you're sure." He turned to face Kaya. "You're going to use your magic to send Trudi, Bill, and Rob back to the *Onion*. I'll stay here with Cassie."

"That isn't possible. I can't send you to your ship," said Kaya.

Ewan's frown deepened. "You better make it possible."

Brine watched the two men nervously. Ewan would love another excuse to attack Kaya, she thought. Only Cassie, and the possibility that Kaya was Brine's father, held him back.

Kaya turned away with an exasperated sigh. "Believe me,

I would like nothing better than to send you all back to your ship. But the movespell requires a spellstone at each end for you to travel between, and you don't have one there. The best I can do is to send you to the village. You'll have to make your own way from there."

"Do you know what he's talking about, Peter?" asked Ewan.

Peter shook his head. "They use magic differently here. But if he says he can only take you to the village, I'd believe him."

"And I believe Peter," said Brine.

Ewan fingered his dagger. "How do we know he won't drop us in a swamp, or in the sea?"

"Because however much I'd like to, it appears my daughter would prefer you to stay alive," snapped Kaya. "I've already taken a risk inviting you into the castle. Wait there."

He swept out of the room and came back moments later holding two pieces of starshell, each set on a gold chain. He offered one to Ewan. The pirate jerked back as if Kaya had thrust a scorpion at him.

"It won't hurt you," said Kaya with a smile.

Ewan snatched the chain. "Only magicians can use starshell."

He jumped as the second starshell repeated his words exactly.

"They are speakstones," said Kaya. "Speak into one and your voice will come out of the other." He offered the second one to Trudi. "If I drop you anywhere deadly, you can tell your friends. You'll still die, of course, but at least they'll be able to avenge you."

Trudi looked at Ewan and waited for him to nod before taking the starshell.

"Now," said Kaya, "if you have no more objections, I'll send you back to the island." His gaze found Brine. "Oshima, you'll stay?"

It was halfway between a command and a question. Brine nodded. "Of course I'm staying. Peter and Tom, too."

Kaya's gaze narrowed. "I'm sorry, but the boy must go back to the island. He has a box full of dangerous, wild magic. I can't allow it to stay in the castle."

"Can't or won't?" asked Ewan quietly.

Peter shoved his box of starshell at Bill. "Take it back to the *Onion*," he said. "It'll be safe there. Now I don't have any magic. Happy, Kaya?"

Kaya's eyes glittered angrily, but he nodded.

Brine let out a slow breath and allowed herself to relax. "Look after Boswell," she whispered to Trudi.

"Don't worry—we'll take care of him. You look after yourself." Trudi cast a meaningful glance over her shoulder at Kaya. "Just because someone says they're somebody, you don't have to believe them," she said, just loud enough for the magus to hear.

Brine's stomach boiled with nerves. Peter and Tom stepped closer to her, one on either side.

It felt strange to let them take charge for a change—strange, and oddly comforting.

"I can't wait to talk," she said, following Kaya out of the room. "I want to know all about you."

"Speaking of knowing things," said Tom. "Does this castle have a library?"

>++++++e

The wind caught Brine's hair as she followed the group out onto the battlements.

"Tell Stella we will come back with her brother," said Peter.

"We'll do our best," promised Trudi. She hugged Brine, then stared into her face as if she'd just noticed something different there. Maybe she had, Brine thought. So much had happened to her in the past years. Even if Kaya was telling her the truth, Oshima the magician's daughter must now be a completely different person from Brine Seaborne the pirate.

Kaya tapped his staff on the stones, and a thin haze of amber light drifted out. "The spell only works for one person at a time," he said. "Stand still."

Bill started to say something, but Brine didn't catch it because the air filled with bright amber light and he vanished.

Brine watched as Trudi and Rob both vanished, too, then she walked to the edge of the battlements and looked over. Wings in the distance were probably teradons; then, looking down, she could see Marfak's Peak, jagged and angry-looking, with broken stones and patches of rising smoke. A beaten dragon, or maybe a defeated magician.

She was home, she thought. Not just that, but she'd found her father, alive and waiting for her. Why wasn't she happy?

She heard the sound of a staff tapping on stone behind her and she turned around. "On a clear day, you can see most of the island from here," said Kaya. "You used to come up here all the time with your mother, and the two of you would spend hours just sitting and looking out at everything." He held out his hand, obviously expecting her to take it, but she drew back. She knew him but she didn't know him, and right now she wasn't sure whether she wanted to trust him.

"Hiri is going to show us the library," Tom called to her. "Do you want to come?"

Brine shook her head. "You go ahead. I'll stay here awhile."

She almost lost her nerve and ran after them as they disappeared inside.

"Oshima?" said Kaya.

Brine remembered that was her name. She clasped her hands behind her.

"What happened to me?" she asked. "I was found in a boat—but how did I end up on the other side of the world? I couldn't have sailed all the way from here to there."

"Your mother sent you." Kaya walked a few paces and stood, his gaze fixed on the circling teradons. "She meant well. You were losing your memory, forgetting us, forgetting your own name. We didn't know what was happening to you, but your mother started to believe the castle was causing it. So she created a movestone. They are supposed to work in pairs, and you travel between them. But your mother used one stone on its own, and you simply disappeared. We had no idea where you'd gone. I spent months searching for you. I used every spell I knew. But Orion's Keep needed me and, in the end, I had to accept that I'd lost you. All I could do was wait and hope you'd eventually find your way back."

And now she had, Brine thought. She gazed out over the battlements.

"Where is my mother?" she asked. "Why isn't she here?"

Kaya turned back to her, his smile gone. "I'm sorry."

Brine felt all the breath go out of her. She gripped the battlement for support. She'd known already, of course—there had to be some reason her mother wasn't here—but she'd managed to keep the thought out of her mind until now. "How?" she asked unsteadily. "How did she die?"

"She fell ill, not long after you disappeared. I'm sorry, Oshima. There are some things even magic cannot cure." Kaya rubbed a hand over his eyes and sighed. "You must have had an adventurous few years."

"Some of it." Homesickness welled up in her, not for this place, but for the sea, for the *Onion*. Right then, she even missed Rob Grosse's smelly underpants. She sat down on the castle battlements, her hands resting back on the warm stones, and, slowly, she began to talk, telling Kaya about her three years on the Minutes Islands, keeping house for Tallis Magus, how

Peter had broken the magician's starshell and they'd run away and joined the *Onion*.

Kaya listened quietly until she got to Marfak West.

"Marfak West?" he echoed sharply.

Brine broke off her story. "He said he'd been here—he told us about Orion's Keep. He didn't mention the volcano, though."

Kaya frowned down at the stones. "He must have taken the name after he left here. He never told us his real name."

This sounded interesting. Brine shifted closer to him. "What happened?"

"It was a long time ago," said Kaya. "You were only a baby, and Orion's Keep had twenty magi. One day we saw a ship." He gave a flicker of a smile. "More of a wreck than a ship, to be honest. We went to investigate and we found a man on board, half dead, his skin burned by the sun, all his hair fallen off, even his eyelashes. At first we couldn't get much sense out of him, but he said he'd come in search of magic. His health returned and he grew stronger—strong enough in the end that he tried to take over the castle and we had to fight him. We beat him, but only just—many of our magi were killed. That's why there are only three of us here now, and that is why we so desperately need the children. They are the ones with the greatest potential, the ones who will be our next magi if only we can find a cure for them."

He turned to face her, his eyes burning bright. "I was beginning to lose hope, Oshima—beginning to think we'd fail

153

and Orion's Keep would fall. But now you have come back and we have hope again."

Brine drew back. The intensity in Kaya's gaze puzzled her—it was something familiar and frightening at the same time. "Why is the castle so important?" she asked. "What are you even doing here?"

Kaya put his hand over hers. "You really don't remember? Orion's Keep is the only thing standing between this island and destruction. If the castle falls, the island will die."

CHAPTER 19

Weather warning: Mysterious whirlpools and waterspouts are causing chaos off the coast of Morning. Islanders are calling for the removal of their ruler, Baron Kaitos. Since the surprise reappearance of Marfak West on Morning some months ago, which resulted in the near-destruction of Baron Kaitos's palace, the island has suffered a drop in trade, and difficult sailing conditions can only make things worse.

(Report submitted to Barnard's Reach by news-scribe)

Peter had never been that interested in books, but even he paused to stare as he entered the library of Orion's Keep. It was right at the bottom of the castle and, in contrast to all the straight lines of the other rooms and corridors, the room was round with a circular table in the middle and bookshelves following the curve of the walls. A carved dragon's head snarled at him from near the ceiling—its tail curling from the lowest shelf—giving the impression that the shelving was made up of the dragon's body, coil on top of coil.

Tom stood beside him, openmouthed. "Where do all these things come from? They look old."

"They are," said Hiri. "We used to trade. There's gold in the sand here, and the magi used to sift it out and melt it down. They had translocation spells that could reach right across the sea to other islands. We don't have enough magic to do it anymore. Worst luck."

Except when Kaya had sent Brine halfway around the world, Peter thought. He wondered how Brine was getting on now.

"What's it like living on a ship?" asked Hiri.

"Smelly," said Tom. "Nobody washes, and we keep getting attacked by giant spiders and things with tentacles. Almost everything that attacks us is either squishy or slimy."

Hiri smiled, and Peter took the chance that the young magus might be in a friendly mood. "How do you do magic? Everyone keeps talking about spellstones, and I never heard of them until I came here."

"Spellstones are the only proper way to use magic," said Ebeko. "Your way of taking raw magic out of a stone with no preparation is completely wrong. I'm surprised you haven't killed yourself with it. Don't you know that wild magic is dangerous?"

All magic was dangerous, Peter thought; that was the whole point of using spellshapes. They forced the magic into a particular pattern so it would cast one spell, and one spell only. And they confined a magician's ability to the number of spellshapes he could remember.

You don't need spellshapes, Marfak West once said. *They're only the rules.* As long as you were clear about what you wanted, magic would respond to your thoughts and change reality to match them. And that was exactly why Peter did need them—because spellshapes put a limit on what he could do, and he needed those limits. Especially now, when he really felt like turning Ebeko into a candlestick.

"It's dangerous," repeated Ebeko stubbornly. "And it's selfish. Instead of creating spellstones for other people to use, you're hoarding all the magic for yourself."

Peter stared around the library uneasily, half expecting to see Marfak West's ghost materialize. "Show me, then," he said. "How do you make a spellstone?"

Marfak West's ghost remained pleasingly nonexistent. Ebeko shook her head, her lips tightly pressed, but Hiri gave Peter a broad grin. "Why not? It's easy."

He took a box off one of the shelves and picked out a narrow sliver of starshell. Peter stared in amazement. They kept starshell unguarded here? Kaya had made him send his box back to the *Onion* when he could help himself to what was here already. This must be a test, to see whether he would steal starshell if he had the chance. Peter sat down, his eyes on Hiri, and kept his hands clasped under the table so he didn't accidentally reach out.

Hiri put the starshell piece on the table and set a pen down next to it. "This is a spellshaper," he said. "The tip is pure gold. So, what you have to do is draw a small amount of magic out of the spellstone into the shaper, and then you draw the spellshape onto the stone."

The tip of the spellshaper glowed amber with magic. Hiri drew a circle carefully onto the starshell. "This is the shape for a finding spell."

Peter knew what a finding spell looked like, but he resisted the urge to say so. He watched as Hiri drew circle after circle. "You have to keep the shape exactly the same each time," he said as he worked. "Do it enough times, and all the magic in the stone will settle into that shape. Then, as the magic replenishes, the new magic is pulled into the shape that's already there; so as long as there's some magic in the stone, the spell will work. Some spells will keep casting constantly; others sit dormant, waiting to be cast. All you have to do then is agitate the magic, and it will cast the spell."

Peter remembered Stella rubbing the heatstones between her hands. He watched Hiri with fascination, and then growing boredom. This was like all those lessons with Tallis Magus, copying spellshapes out over and over onto sheets of paper.

Hiri sat back. "That should be enough. I chose the finding spell because it works with a single stone. A lot of spellstones work in pairs, like speakstones and movestones. You need one at each end point, and you move either your voice or yourself between them."

"Can you write more than one spell into a stone?" Peter asked.

"You can, but it's not recommended, not unless the spells are related and you know a lot about magic." Hiri held the starshell out to Tom. "Try it."

Tom rubbed the piece between his hands. "Show me the most interesting books in the library."

A blade of amber light shot from the starshell and hit the floor in the corner of the room.

Peter grinned. "And that is a perfect example of magic not doing what you expect. Where do all these spellstones come from?"

Hiri shrugged. "They're just here. You can keep that one, Tom, if you like."

"Thanks." Tom slipped the piece into his notebook. "If you don't mind, I'd like to visit the children again."

"I'll come with you," said Ebeko, getting up. It appeared that the magi didn't want to leave either of them on their own. A sure sign they were hiding something, Peter thought. He waited until they'd gone, and then he sat back in his chair. "So," he said. "Orion's Keep is named after a dragon . . ."

CHAPTER 20

After the last eruption of Marfak's Peak destroyed half the island, the surviving magi knew that the only way to protect Apcaron was to prevent Marfak from ever erupting again. And so they built Orion's Keep, named after a dragon and full of magic.

(from THE HISTORY OF ORION'S KEEP)

Y ou know the story of the two dragons," said Kaya. "Of course you do—you're a storyteller at heart. So you'll know that every story is based on truth."

His words were so close to what Brine had said herself many times that she wondered if she's been echoing him all along. "But there are no dragons," she said, hoping Kaya would contradict her.

Except for Boswell, who was probably driving everyone on the ship mad right now. Brine hoped the others wouldn't take too long getting back to the *Onion*.

Kaya sat down on the edge of the battlements, seemingly oblivious to the fact that there was nothing but a death-defyingly long drop behind him. "No, there's no dragon, but the volcano is a real danger. Before this castle was built, Marfak's Peak used to erupt without warning and each eruption was worse than the last. The magi knew that if they didn't do something, the whole island would be swallowed up by lava. And so they built Orion's Keep, with one purpose—to keep Marfak contained. They built a castle, as high up on the slopes of Marfak's Peak as they could manage. They filled the walls with spellstones, all of them impressed with the same spell, to push down on the volcano and suppress the fire within it. And all the spells slowly pushed the castle into the air until it stopped right over the volcano peak."

Boswell's third law of motion—for every action there is an equal and opposite reaction. Pushing down on the volcano lifted the castle up. "It seems like a lot of effort," said Brine. "Couldn't they have used their spells to turn the volcano into an ordinary mountain, or a fish?"

Kaya laughed softly. "A fish the size of a mountain? No, if there was another way, they'd have done it. This was the best, the only way. Every magus since has continued the work of the first magi, renewing and maintaining the spellstones that hold the castle together and keep Marfak's Peak in check."

Brine tried to imagine what would happen to the insides of a volcano if it were kept from erupting for over a hundred years. It would be like putting a lid on a cooking pot—and she'd seen enough of Trudi's pots boil over to know what that was like. "You can't just keep doing this," she said. "Sooner or later Marfak's Peak will erupt anyway, and it'll be a hundred times worse."

Kaya frowned. "I've spent my whole life here. Trust me: I know what I'm doing."

His voice stirred something inside Brine. She had trusted him once, she thought, and a memory flashed across her vision—her hand grasping his as she followed him through the stone passages of Orion's Keep.

She leaned forward eagerly. "We can help," she said. "I know you and Peter got off badly, but he really is good at magic. And Tom knows a lot about science, and Cassie . . . Well, Cassie can hit things, which probably isn't what you need."

She wondered if she should tell him about Boswell, too. But Peter had wanted to investigate dragons, so better to leave that to him.

Kaya smiled and started to get up, but then he doubled over, coughing.

"It's nothing," said Kaya, waving Brine away. "My work here has been demanding of late. That's all." He drew in a ragged breath and gripped her hands tightly. "You know what the hardest thing is? Waiting. Year after year, not knowing whether you'll ever see a person again, not knowing if they're alive or what's happening to them. All you can do is hope that one day, somehow, they'll find their way home."

Brine didn't know where to look. Kaya expected her to stay, she thought. Of course he did—she'd traveled halfway around the world to find him, so how could she possibly leave now? And he needed her help. How could she tell him that she longed for the open sea around her, the excitement of never knowing what was over the horizon or what the next day would bring?

Kaya straightened up. "I'd like to try a few experiments with you if you don't mind. Your friend Tom could help, too. We have certain toys and puzzles designed to get the mind working. You've recovered far better than the children here. If we can find out why, it may help us find a cure."

"Of course." Brine took his arm as they walked back to the steps. Helping with experiments sounded like fun, and if nothing else it would keep her mind off bigger problems— like what in the wide oceans was she going to do.

If you are reading this journal, then I am dead. Unless you have taken it without my permission, in which case I am very angry. Put it back at once.

This is our first day in Orion's Castle. Cassie is still sleeping. Rob, Bill, and Trudi have returned to the island. After a brief overview of the library, I have commenced my plan of investigating the mystery of the sick children. Here are my results:

Phase 1: Experiments

<u>Reading to them</u>—no response

<u>Singing to them</u>—Ren, the youngest boy, moved away, but this may be because of the quality of my singing

<u>Food</u>—they ate if food was offered but did not appear to mind, or even notice, what they were eating. I gave them fish and pieces of meat and vegetable and then some sweet stuff—I'm not sure what it was—and they ate everything as if it were the same

<u>Toys and games</u>—there are many. The children showed no interest, with one exception (see below)

Phase 2: Research

I talked to Ebeko. I don't think she likes us being here. She watched me the whole time I was with the children, and I am fairly certain she doesn't trust me (this is supposed to be a scientific journal, and so I should point out that I have no evidence other than her constant watching and scowling).

I asked her what the magi had already done to investigate a cure. She replied that Kaya "was trying."

Then I asked why Kaya kept taking children when he knew they may end up suffering from the same malady?

She replied: "The castle needs more magi to survive."

I have the strong impression that there were many more magi here until quite recently, but something happened to them. When I asked Ebeko about this, she said I'd have to talk to Kaya.

I noticed that every time Ebeko mentions Kaya, she loses her frown for a moment. I think she likes him.

Phase 3: Kaya

Discussions with Ebeko were interrupted when Kaya and Brine arrived to conduct some experiments. Kaya wishes to establish whether Brine's memory loss is connected to the children's current malady. As this will aid my investigation, I readily agreed to participate and also to document the results.

The tests consisted first of answering questions. Kaya is keen to find out how much of Brine's old life she remembers. He calls Brine "Oshima," which sounds strange but is apparently her real name. Next Kaya gave each of us a strange puzzle box. Each side consists of sliding panels of different shapes and sizes that you can move around. If you get the right combination, Kaya said, the box will open. It is a test of memory and intelligence.

The box was certainly intriguing, but most intriguing was Ren's reaction. Finally, he paid attention to what I was doing, and he tried to take the box and open it. I let him play with it for a short while before he lost interest and dropped it. Kaya says Ren does occasionally become aware of what's around him for short periods. I have kept the box for further study.

Kaya is the biggest puzzle of all. He is patient, kind to the children, and Brine seems to like him. The magi have devoted their lives to protecting the island, but the islanders clearly don't like or trust the magi. And then there's the problem of the children. What kind of man would continue to bring children here when they are all losing their minds to the same illness?

I need to think about this. Right now,

however, thinking is giving me a headache and I
ought to rest. I'll take a break from investigating
and try to solve the puzzle box.

I'm sure I meant to write more, but I can't
quite remember what.

CHAPTER 21

SPECIAL DRAGON SNACKS

One handful of giant spider legs

Oil (something strongly flavored like fish oil is good)

Salt

Chili pepper (lots)

Heat the oil in a large pan. Season the spider legs with salt and plenty of chili pepper. (No need to clean them first. Dragons don't care.) Fry in the oil until blackened and crispy. Cover in more chili pepper. Remember to wash your hands after feeding your dragon.

(from COOKING UP A STORME—
THE RECIPES OF A GOURMET PIRATE)

The day wore on. While Brine and Tom continued memory experiments with Kaya, Peter explored the castle. Hiri and Ebeko took turns following him about "in case he needed anything." What Peter really needed was them to go away. The servants and guards in the castle all avoided him politely, answering questions when he spoke to them but clearly not wanting to be around him. "What's in here?" asked

Peter, trying a door on one of the four towers and finding it locked.

"Nothing," said Hiri. "The stairs are crumbling. That tower's been locked for years. With so few of us in the castle, we don't need the extra space and we don't have time to deal with repairs."

Hiri had plenty of time to follow a guest around the castle for a whole afternoon, though, Peter thought, making his way back inside.

Much of the castle did look like it was in need of repair. Carpets that were worn through to holes in places, broken furniture, and when Peter ran his hands over the walls in the main hall, he found a whole patch of loose stones.

"What are you going to do when the castle falls apart?" he asked.

Hiri shrugged unhappily. "It won't."

It would, Peter thought. The volcano wasn't dead, Marfak West had said, it was dormant, and one day it would erupt again. That time might be sooner than any of them thought. It was a good thing Brine was back because Kaya really needed someone to come up with a plan.

▸┅┽┼╫┝❤

As afternoon turned to evening, they all gathered in the main hall to eat. Kaya had filled the long table with an amazing array of food but none of them ate. Peter sat between Brine and Tom, watching Brine pick unenthusiastically at a plate of greens. Tom spent the whole time fiddling with his wooden puzzle box.

"Each surface is made up of sliding panels," he said. "If you line the panels up just right, the box will open. It's quite fascinating."

It didn't seem fascinating at all to Peter. The shadows slowly darkened as the sun sank lower outside. Sunset, Peter thought. That was when Marapi would declare that their rescue had failed. What would happen to Stella then?

Then the door slammed open and Ewan Hughes came in, wearing a clean shirt and a giant grin. "Cassie woke up," he said. "She's back asleep now, but she's looking better."

Tom glanced up from his puzzle box. "That's nice."

Peter kicked him. "Tom, pay attention. Have you spoken to Trudi, Ewan? Did they make it back to the village?"

Ewan's grin spread even wider. "Those speakstone things really work. Trudi said they went to the village and explained what had happened. Stella was there, she said, and—Is that roasted dinosaur?"

"Help yourself," said Kaya drily as Ewan stuffed meat into his mouth.

Ewan wiped his hands on his trousers. "Anyway, Marapi's back in charge at the village, but we'll sort that out once Cassie's up on her feet. Trudi, Rob, and Bill are back on the *Onion*. Trudi said to tell you not to worry about Boswell."

"Who's Boswell?" asked Kaya.

"The cat," said Brine quickly. "It's my job to look after him."

Peter was surprised how easily Brine had lied, and how easily Kaya appeared to believe her. He glanced at Tom, but Tom had his head down over his puzzle box again.

Ewan swallowed another mouthful of meat. "I guess we're staying the night, then. Where do we sleep?"

The next morning, Brine woke, wondering why everything felt so strange, then she realized what it was: She wasn't moving. Instead of a swaying hammock, she had a whole bed to herself—a whole bedroom, in fact, at least twice the size of Cassie's cabin on board the *Onion*.

Over breakfast—real breakfast, not last night's leftovers—Ewan reported that Cassie was feeling better. "Still not on her feet," he said, piling a plate up with orange cheese, "but another day's rest should do the trick. You three can amuse yourselves here today, can't you?"

Brine glanced at Peter and nodded. Tom ignored her, eating with one hand and sliding panels about on his puzzle box with the other. Brine snatched it from him and slapped it down on the table. "Tom!"

"What?" He blinked at her. "Sorry. What were you saying?"

Kaya stood up. "Oshima, I was thinking we should tidy up one of those rooms for you to have as your own. Do you want to choose one?"

It didn't feel quite so strange to Brine when he called her Oshima now, and that was strange in itself—that she could accept a new name so quickly. She got up from the table. She didn't really want to choose a room as if she was going to stay here forever, but it was a chance to spend some more time with Kaya. "Peter? Tom?" she asked.

"Still eating," said Peter.

Tom yawned. "Actually, I'm really tired. I think I might go back to bed."

He wandered out. Brine stared after him in surprise and then looked down to see his notebook on his chair. "Tom never leaves his notebook behind," she said.

Ebeko snatched it off her. "I'll give it back to him."

She hurried after Tom. "But—" began Brine.

Kaya rested his hand on her shoulder, wheezing heavily. "Ebeko will take care of it. Don't worry. There's a very nice room in the south tower, hasn't been used in years. Come and see."

Casting Peter a despairing glance, Brine followed.

Kaya kept her so busy for the rest of the day that Brine barely saw Tom or Peter. She ached with the need to talk to them, but Kaya was always with her and Hiri and Ebeko took it in turns hanging about so that conversation was impossible.

"How's Cassie?" Brine asked Ewan.

"Sleeping again. Her leg looks completely normal now. Trudi said to tell you the cat's missing you."

The cat meaning Boswell, of course. Brine missed the little dragon, too. As soon as Cassie was back on her feet, they should go and fetch him, she thought. Maybe she'd like the castle better if she had Boswell here. It was worth a try, because Kaya clearly expected her to stay. It was as if he still saw her the way she must have been three years ago. But a lot had changed since then, and Brine wasn't the same person. Maybe Kaya would understand that in time. Or maybe in time Brine would start feeling like she belonged here again. She had to try, because she was Kaya's daughter and he needed her. That was the whole point of a family, wasn't it—being there for people when they needed you?

She went to bed in her new, big room halfway up the south tower, but she couldn't sleep. She lay there for maybe an hour, and then, sighing, she got up, pulled her clothes on, and slipped out the door.

►⊹⊹╫╫●

Peter couldn't sleep. He was used to lying in a hammock with Brine right above him, the sound of snoring pirates echoing back and forth. This room was too big, too quiet.

Someone opened his door a crack. Ebeko, checking on him, Peter thought, though it was too dark to see. He lay still, breathing steadily, pretending to sleep until the door shut quietly. He stayed where he was for a while after that, then he got up and sat by the door until he was sure he couldn't hear any noises from the castle. Kaya was hiding something, he was sure. Perhaps it was because of his experience with Marfak West, but Peter didn't trust any magician who appeared friendly.

On tiptoe, he slipped out of the room and ran to the stairs that led to the battlements. He didn't stop to see whether Brine or Tom was still awake. Someone was bound to notice if they all left their rooms, but Peter was used to sneaking about the *Onion*. He could do this better on his own.

A few torches burned in the corridors and on the stairs, but their light seemed to push the shadows together, so in certain places you couldn't see a thing. Peter kept to the darkest patches, walking slowly so his feet didn't make any noise on the steps.

Above the battlements, the sky stretched dark and wide, and the constellation of Orion the dragon burned fiercely, every star looking like a tiny stab wound in the night. Peter put his hands flat on the wall and tried to feel for the tingle of magic. If the castle walls were full of spellstones, he should be able to feel the magic coming off them. It took him several seconds of concentration before he caught it: just the faintest tickling against his palms. It ought to be more than that. Nothing here made proper sense. It was like Tom's puzzle box—if they could only get the pieces in the right order, the whole thing might open up, but at the moment it felt like there were several pieces still missing.

A door opened. Peter shrank back into the shadows as a guard came out, looked around briefly, and went back inside. Four towers, Peter thought, and one of them was kept locked. He flexed his fingers and felt the tingle of magic in his palm. He wondered briefly whether he should go back to the library and take more starshell, but that would increase the risk of getting caught. The little bit of magic he carried with him would be enough.

Peter had become better at opening locks since the first time he'd tried it. This one only took a couple of minutes, and that included having to stop and hide once when another guard came out.

The door swung back soundlessly and smoothly, considering it had been locked for years and the hinges should have rusted shut. Peter took a torch from its bracket and hoped that no one would notice it was gone; then, tentatively, he opened the door and stepped through.

Back on the *Onion*, Trudi Storme was also having trouble sleeping.

Yesterday's conversation in the village hadn't gone well. Marapi hadn't won yet, but she'd acted as if she had—and so had most of the village. Trudi wished she'd brought Cerro and Stella back to the *Onion*, but she wasn't quick-thinking like Cassie or good at making plans like Brine. She was just herself and she'd been worried, fed up, and had wanted to get back to the ship as quickly as possible.

A mournful howl issued from the galley, followed by the

scrabble of claws on wood. Boswell was trying to dig his way out again. Brine had said to look after him, but Trudi wondered how long they should keep the dragon locked up in there. She slid out of her hammock and padded barefoot to the door.

"Sorry," she whispered. "They're not back yet. I'm sure everyone will be back tomorrow, and then we'll let you out. Probably." She hoped so. Ewan hadn't contacted her through the speakstone, so she knew nothing had changed. He'd tell her if anything had happened.

Boswell howled some more. Trudi put on her stern face and rapped on the door. "It's no good carrying on like that. You have to stay in the galley where it's safe. And don't set fire to anything, either."

The dragon noises stopped. Trudi stood by the door for a while. "Are you all right in there?"

Nothing.

Maybe he really had set fire to something. Trudi smiled, then her eyes widened in panic and she jerked the door open.

A silver-green streak flew past her head. Trudi yelled and ducked, her shout bringing pirates tumbling out of their hammocks.

"Shut the hatch!" Trudi screamed. "Stop that dragon!"

Too late: Boswell shot out of the hatch. It slammed shut behind him. Trudi threw it back open and saw Tim Burre's surprised face looking down at her. "I think Boswell just flew past me."

"I know." A tiny dark shape paused between sea and sky, and a tongue of fire flared briefly. Trudi groaned.

"What do we do now?" asked Tim Burre. "Brine's going to be furious."

Never mind Brine. Trudi was suddenly thinking of all the things that might happen to one small dragon on that island. She dashed back down to the galley and grabbed a packet off the shelf. Then she ran up the stairs. "Crispy chili spider legs," she said, waving the greasy bag at Tim Burre. "They're Boswell's favorite. Bill, get Peter's starshell; the smell of magic might attract Boswell back. We're going after him." As an afterthought she tossed Kaya's speakstone to Tim Burre. "You better keep this in case Ewan gets in touch. Whatever you do, don't tell him Boswell is missing. Who wants to come with me?"

▸┉┼┼╢●

Peter was about halfway down the stairs when the cold hit him. It seemed to come from every direction at once, slamming into his bones and filling him with a dread that pinned him to the spot. He didn't know what was at the bottom of these steps, but he knew he didn't want to find out. He wanted to turn around now and go back to bed where it was safe and warm.

The moment he began to turn around, the cold eased. Not by much, but it was enough that Peter stopped. The feeling of panic wasn't coming from inside himself, he realized: It was all around him. He put a hand on the wall and jerked away with a hiss of pain. He hadn't felt much magic in the castle walls yet, but it was here now, buzzing against his flesh as if hundreds of angry, stinging insects were trying to get free. The whole stairway was infested with spells—spells that set his heart pounding with fear and made his legs shake at the thought of taking one more step.

Gripping the torch in both hands, Peter held it out in front of him and forced his feet to move down to the next step. Even though he knew what was causing this, it didn't make it any easier.

But then the decision to be less afraid seemed to work all by itself. The next step down was easier, and the next one easier still. *Don't think; just keep walking.*

The stairs ended in a corridor so cold and dark that it felt like no one had walked there for centuries. Peter's footsteps sounded muffled. He wasn't sure whether he was heading into the castle or to the outside of it. He walked slowly, not quite trusting what he could see by the flickering torchlight.

Then, unexpectedly, the torch struck something solid right across the corridor. Peter paused in surprise. As far as he could see, the corridor continued on as before, but there was definitely something in the way.

He felt around and made out the outline of a door and then a series of locks. Good old-fashioned, unmagical locks. Peter almost laughed. Somebody had gone to the trouble of making the door invisible but not magically fastening it as well.

The starshell in his hand held just enough power. He pushed and prodded at the locks until the various mechanisms clicked and, one by one, they came undone. The door didn't budge at first, but he shoved it hard, and it finally came unstuck and slammed back.

The door opened onto nothing. Looking down, Peter saw empty sky and the land far below. For a moment he clung to the wall while his heart pounded. Why have a door that led nowhere? If you were worried about people falling, why not just wall up the end of the corridor so that nobody could get through?

A thin gust of wind came up around his feet. The cold woke his senses. Carefully, he knelt and felt out into the emptiness as far as he dared. There was definitely a hole, but as he leaned out, his hands found stone on the other side. The corridor continued invisibly. Whatever was on the other side must be very important indeed for somebody to go to this much trouble to hide it.

Or there was nothing there and these were all half-broken spells.

The thought came into his head, but Peter didn't believe it for a moment. He stood at the edge of the hole, looking down, then he drew in a deep breath and jumped.

His feet landed solidly and he cried out in relief. In the same moment, as if he'd passed through the boundaries of the illusion, he saw what was ahead.

Some small part of him was not surprised at all. The rest

of him was shouting in horror. Kaya had lied. The magus knew that dragons were more than stories. He knew they'd lived on this island. Pieces of starshell in the walls of the castle could never have kept it afloat for this long. Only one thing could have produced the amount of magic the castle needed.

And there were four of them here.

Eggs. Dragon eggs.

CHAPTER 22

Dragons, it is said, live in volcanoes. While other creatures would perish in the heat, dragons thrive in it. Fire is like water to them. Once, dragons nested on all the islands in the Western Ocean. But magi, greedy for their eggs, killed them all one by one. They drove dragons from their nests and stole their eggs before they could hatch, and one year the dragons did not return to nest.

(from THE HISTORY OF ORION'S KEEP)

Peter wasn't in his bed. Brine gazed into the empty room with a mixture of concern and annoyance. Trust him to go wandering when she wanted to talk to him.

Unless, of course, he hadn't just wandered off, and something had happened to him. Peter did have a talent for getting himself into trouble. He'd said he was going to look for dragons. Maybe he'd found one and it had eaten him.

Panic flooded her even though she knew there was no need to worry. Peter was probably in Tom's room next door. She banged on the door, then wrenched it open.

"Peter . . ."

He wasn't there. Tom sat in bed, his notebook balanced on his knees and the puzzle box lying beside him.

Honestly, he was obsessed with that thing. Brine snatched it up and threw it onto the floor. "Tom! Peter is missing. Remember Peter? Your friend."

"Brine . . . ," said Tom.

She stamped on the box. She put all her frustration into it until it felt like she was stamping her way out of prison. She didn't stop until the box was in pieces. "I'm sick of puzzles," she said. "I'm sick of not knowing what to do. That thing was taking over your mind—you even forgot your notebook at breakfast."

"I didn't," said Tom.

"Yes, you did. I saw you."

"You saw me pretend," said Tom.

Brine stopped, her mouth open. Tom grinned at her and squirmed across the bed so he could sit on the edge. "I wanted to see what the magi would do if they thought I was losing my memory. They should be panicking and trying to get me out of the castle before I forget everything. Instead, they watched me, but they seemed more interested than anything. I even wrote in my notebook that I was forgetting things and left it for Ebeko to read. She didn't say a word, though she watched me like an eagle after that. It was almost like they were expecting it to happen, and they were only surprised that it happened so fast."

Brine thought back to the morning, Ebeko following Tom out the door. "Maybe they didn't really notice," she said uncertainly. "They don't know you like we do." That had to be it—because if it wasn't, it meant Kaya knew far more about the children's illness than he was telling them. She stirred the bits of puzzle box with her foot.

Something glittered amid the broken pieces.

"What's that?" Tom asked. Brine bent to pick it up.

Whatever it was, it was coated all over in gold, and the gold was engraved with overlapping shapes forming patterns that drew Brine's gaze and made her feel like she was being pulled out of herself and into them.

Starshell, she thought. Engraved with who-knew-what spellshapes. "We need Peter," she said, but Peter wasn't here. Brine gathered up the bits of broken wood; it was all she could think of to do. She felt tears pricking her eyes. "What do we do now?"

"Well, we could tell Ewan," said Tom. "And he could wake Kaya and have a big fight. Or . . . wait a minute. Did you say Peter was missing?"

Brine nodded. "I bet he's gone exploring without us. He's going to get into trouble."

"Where would a magician go in a place like this?" asked Tom. He smiled. "There's a box of starshell in the library. Let's start there."

The four eggs sat in nests of sand. They were smaller than Boswell's egg, and while Boswell's egg had been covered in a thick layer of ice, these shone with a warm light. Peter reached out instinctively to touch one of them before realizing what he was doing and drawing his hand back sharply. When Boswell had hatched, the explosion had torn Marfak West's ship apart. Four eggs together would destroy the whole castle and everyone in it.

Peter rubbed his hands across his face, his thoughts whirling. He'd have to talk to Cassie, and he'd need to tell Brine, too—tell her that the home she'd dreamed of was built on lies and stolen dragon eggs—and that her father was the biggest liar of all.

But then . . . maybe Kaya didn't know? The first magi, the people who'd built the castle over a hundred years ago, were the ones who'd filled the walls with starshell. They would have been the ones who put the eggs here. It was possible that the three magi who remained had no idea what was hidden just beneath their feet.

But even as Peter was thinking it, he knew it couldn't be true. Hiri and Ebeko might not know, but Kaya definitely did. Kaya knew every stone of this castle. He knew what was here and he'd been hiding it. That was why he'd wanted to send Peter back to the *Onion* and why he'd made sure someone was watching him every minute. He must have been afraid the whole time that Peter would discover his secret.

Well, now the secret was out. Peter clenched his fists hard.

How could Kaya have done this? To know that four dragon eggs waited here, unhatched, to draw off their magic and never allow the dragons to live while all the time, the amount of magic in the world kept increasing. If Kaya knew anything about dragons, he should know that the world needed them.

The air in the room felt too hot, too heavy. Brine liked Kaya. She thought he was trying to save the island, and she'd be devastated to learn the truth.

Somebody had to tell her, though. Peter left the room and fastened all the locks on the door as best he could. It didn't look quite right, but he didn't think anyone would be coming down here to check. He'd talk to Ewan and Cassie first, and then he'd have to tell Brine and Tom.

Quickly, not caring that his footsteps echoed along the stone corridor and stairway, he ran back the way he'd come.

He stepped out onto the battlements and stopped, his heart sinking.

Kaya stood a few paces away, alone. The tip of his staff glowed.

"You've broken Orion's Law," he said.

Strangely, the magus looked sad. Peter had expected him to look angry, or guilty, anything but this weary expression, as if the weight of the whole island had just landed on his shoulders.

Some of Peter's rage dissipated. "I know what you're hiding here. Do you want to talk about this before I tell the others?"

"There's nothing to talk about," said Kaya.

"Yes, there is. You're keeping dragon eggs. You knew all along that dragons really existed. You could have brought them back, but you're keeping them, using their magic. Why?" Peter took a step forward. He wished he'd gone to the library for starshell after all—or maybe it was just as well that he didn't, because his imagination suggested several things he wanted to do right now, and none of them were pretty . . .

Kaya stood completely still. He was a magus, Peter thought. He of all people ought to understand. "Dragons balance the amount of magic in the world. Now they are gone, and there is too much magic. That means giant spiders, mirages, and monsters. You think you need the eggs for their magic, but we need dragons so much more."

"There have always been monsters and magic," said Kaya. "Dragons are best left to the stories now. I'm sorry. I'll take care of Oshima, I promise."

A spellshape flared to life around Peter's feet, and he realized too late what Kaya was doing. "Wait!" he shouted.

The whole world turned black, and for a second or two Peter felt like he was floating and the only thing he could feel was a final, faint crackle of magic from the starshell in his hand. Then his feet hit something solid, and the night rushed back in around him.

He appeared to be standing on a small patch of land in the middle of a lake. The water looked thick and dark and undulated softly. When Peter moved his feet, they squelched, and he felt water seeping into his shoes.

Then he heard a snarl.

▶—++))+●

The library was empty. Brine shut the door behind her and put her lamp onto the table. Her palms were damp. "He's not here," she said needlessly. "Now what?" This brought back memories of stealing into Tallis Magus's library by night, and she knew what that had led to.

Tom held up the spellstone that Hiri had given him. "When I tried it before, I asked it to show me the most interesting books in the library and the spell hit the floor, over there somewhere. I thought it had gone wrong, but let's try again." He rubbed the starshell between his hands. "Show me the most interesting books in the library."

Amber light burst out and speared straight into the floor. Brine squeaked in fright. It had worked—Tom had used magic. She tried to take the spellstone off him. "Let me have a go."

Tom closed his hand over the stone. "We've got to conserve magic. We don't know how many spells this thing has got left in it or how long it will take to recharge."

Brine crossed to the door. Everything was quiet outside, so Peter couldn't have been caught yet. "All right," she said. "Quickly, though."

She hurried to the corner of the room where the spell had hit and pulled back the rug. The floor was all in squares beneath, each one looking solid and solidly fixed. Brine's heart sank. Tom was so certain something was hidden here that she'd been sure she'd find a trapdoor or secret passage.

Tom knelt beside her and started pushing at the squares.

"What are you doing?" asked Brine.

"I think this might be like the puzzle boxes." He pushed down hard on two of the blocks together. Something clicked but nothing moved. Tom hit the floor. "Come on—open up!"

The squares weren't all lined up in rows. If you looked at a certain set in the right way, they formed a triangle. Or a volcano. And another block, higher up and to the right, was slightly smaller than the others. "That one," she said, pointing.

"A volcano and a castle. Got it!" Tom pressed down on the smaller block.

At the same time, Brine reached in and pushed the set of blocks that formed the volcano.

The section of floor sank down so quickly that both lost their balance and fell against each other. Brine picked herself up and bent to peer into the hole underneath. "Tom, I think we did it. There's something in here."

She put her hand in and felt the edges of a box. Holding her breath, she eased the lid off and started lifting out books, passing each one back to Tom. Most of them were handwritten, and some weren't even proper books, just stacks of paper held together with string.

"The most interesting books in the library," said Tom with a grin.

The two of them read fast. Columns of figures, journal entries, notes about magic. Brine read with a growing sense of dread. Here it was, staring back at her in faded ink: everything that was wrong with the castle.

Then she noticed that Tom was staring at one book, reading a page over and over again, and his suntanned face redder and angrier than she'd ever seen it.

"What have you found?" she asked.

Tom pushed his hair back and slapped the book down on the floor. "Something I hoped wouldn't be here at all." His voice shook with the full force of a librarian's disapproval. "This is Kaya's notebook."

CHAPTER 23

Magic may seem unnatural to the ignorant, but it is merely another form of energy, and energy can easily be converted from one form into another. It happens all the time in spellcasting—magic is transformed into light or heat or healing. The question is, how do we turn ordinary energy into magic? We need to start with the right type of energy.

(from RECORDS OF ORION'S KEEP—
First Magus Belen Kaya)

Three pirates crept through the undergrowth of Dragon Island.

"Boswell," called Trudi. She rattled Peter's box of starshell gently. "Who's a good dragon? We've got magic for you. And spider legs. Bos-weeeeeeell!"

She paused and listened. There were plenty of noises— branches rustling, birds hooting and calling, but nothing sounded like a dragon. She rattled the starshell again.

"You're going to break that," said Bill.

A bird shot out of a nearby tree, and Rob whipped out his

sword, looking around hopefully for something to fight. Trudi hushed him and held her breath, listening hard.

She'd discovered something in the past hour—she didn't like the dark. She wasn't afraid of it, exactly: It just made her feel uneasy. On the *Onion* it was fine because you had the stars to navigate by and the open sea reflected back the moonlight, so it was rarely completely dark. But on land, especially on a strange island full of trees, it was a different matter. Every direction looked the same, and every tree looked like it had a monster hiding behind it.

If she were a baby dragon who'd just learned to fly, where would she go? Trudi wished she had a better imagination. She wasn't a dragon: She was just a pirate who was going to get into a mountain of trouble over this.

She turned around slowly. The trees all merged into the same black mass. "Have you got any idea where we are now?" she asked.

Rob scratched behind his ears with his sword blade. "I thought you were in charge of directions."

"No, I'm in charge of finding Boswell. You two were supposed to be watching where we were going."

"You didn't tell us that," grumbled Rob.

So now they were lost, too. Just great. Trudi swallowed back her rising panic and tried to ignore the voice in her head that told her this was all her fault. She was a cook, not an explorer. What did she think she was doing here?

"What would Cassie do?" asked Bill.

Trudi told her head to shut up and straightened her shoulders. "It doesn't matter what Cassie would do because Cassie isn't here. We are." She wasn't just any old cook. She was a cook on board the *Onion*. She was part of the fearsomest crew that had ever sailed the eight oceans. She had faced monsters and magicians and librarians. She wasn't going to let a little thing like the dark frighten her.

A branch snapped. Trudi jumped, her heart pounding. All right, maybe the dark did frighten her, but she had a dragon to find and she'd do it whether she was afraid or not.

"This way," she said, picking a direction at random, and she set off.

Two seconds later someone stepped out from behind a tree. Trudi yelled and leaped back, and then she saw who it was. She lowered her sword—she hadn't even realized she'd drawn it. "Stella. What are you doing here?"

Stella crossed her arms. "Getting away from the village. Marapi wanted to lock me up with Cerro. He's pretty much her prisoner now, since you failed to rescue Ren."

"We didn't fail," said Trudi. "It's just taking a little longer than anticipated. Cassie will bring him back. Don't worry."

Stella shrugged angrily. "It doesn't matter. I still have the balloon. I'm going to go to the castle and look for Ren myself. I don't need your help."

She glared, daring them to disagree. Any minute now she'd walk away, Trudi thought, and if she got hurt in the dark, it would be their fault. They were the ones who'd started all this.

An idea squirmed into life in her mind. Stella wouldn't accept help, but maybe she'd offer it. "We're in a bit of a mess," she said. "I think we may be lost, and Boswell is missing."

Stella turned back to them. "Boswell is missing? Where is he?"

"If we knew that," said Rob, "he wouldn't be missing, would he? He flew off the ship. He's on the island somewhere. Where would a dragon go?"

Stella kicked her feet back and forth. "The volcano, maybe," said Stella. "Or the lizard swamp. It's warm there." She hesitated, torn between stomping off on her own and helping them find the dragon.

"He's never been off the ship before," said Trudi. "I hope those teradons don't find him."

She immediately wished she hadn't said it as she imagined Boswell pursued by a flock of vengeful flying dinosaurs.

Stella gave an exasperated sigh. "None of you should be allowed off your ship. You're a menace. Well, I guess I might as well stay with you, seeing as I'm out here anyway. Shall we try the swamp?"

Trudi gestured for her to lead on. That hadn't gone too badly. She wasn't just a cook, after all. She could talk to people and persuade them to help, even if they didn't really want to. The darkness didn't seem so bad now. That large tree up ahead that looked like a dinosaur was only a misshapen trunk. She could do this.

The tree moved.

"Is that a dinosaur?" asked Bill.

><+++)(<●

P eter turned around slowly. Eyes watched him from every-where. Various shades, ranging from yellow to bright green, and all of them narrowed to hungry slits. Peter's breath came faster. He took a step back, and his feet splashed into water. The patch of ground he was standing on was so small, he could cross it in six steps. The starshell in his hand was cold, empty of magic right when he needed it most. He picked up a tree branch and swung it around his head. The end was rotten and fell off, but the rest would do as a weapon.

A lizard about the length of Peter's forearm slithered out of the swamp and snapped at his foot. Peter kicked it away, picked up a stone, and threw it into the murky water. The swamp turned into a mass of thrashing bodies as every lizard within reach converged on the spot. Well, at least that gave him some idea of how many creatures there were—a lot of them, and not just small ones. Some of them looked bigger than he was.

"It could be worse," he said out loud in case that helped—but it didn't. He was trapped in the middle of a swamp full of hungry reptiles: How could it possibly be worse?

A brown back broke the water right by him. Peter jumped

back as the reptile burst out of the swamp and knocked him flat. The monster landed on top of him, pinning him to the ground. Peter tried to push its jaw out of his face, but it was too heavy to move. It snarled and snapped, dripping swamp water everywhere.

Peter had faced certain death before. Not on his own, though. Brine and Tom would never even know what had happened to him. He strained at the monster with both hands, but his arms were starting to give out. The jaws edged closer.

Then the night filled with a flurry of wings and flame, and something roared right in his ear. The monster on top of him leaped back as if Peter had forced it away with magic.

"Boswell!" Peter shouted.

How had Boswell gotten here? Peter's sudden elation at seeing the dragon changed to terror. Boswell was going to be killed; he couldn't win a fight against something that was twenty times his size. But the monster, which could have eaten Boswell in a single bite, let out an enormous sneeze and rolled off Peter and back into the swamp. Boswell chased it, blowing out more fire. The monster cowered in the water, sneezed again, and sank under the surface.

Peter got up, shaking, feeling himself all over for injuries. It was several moments before he could say anything.

Boswell landed on his feet.

"Well done," Peter croaked.

A muffled sneeze sounded from underwater, and a few bubbles rose to the surface. Could a swamp monster be allergic to magic? Allergic or not, it would be back, Peter thought. He had to get out of here. He stepped into the swamp and immediately sank to his waist in warm water. The only way out of here was to swim. In the dark and surrounded by reptiles that seemed to think that he was a special food delivery. Something chewed his shoe, and he scrabbled hastily back onto the patch of land and sat down right in the center, his knees drawn up to his chin.

"Having fun?" a voice inquired.

Magic is creative energy; it is potential: a spark of life waiting to happen—and who has more potential, more creativity than children?

The original spell designed to draw creativity out and capture it worked too well. The subject needed too much time to recover. Based on my findings, I have created several modified spellstones and am ready to try them. What's needed now is something to keep the subjects engaged and using their creative minds so that the spellstone can have maximum effect. Some sort of toy or puzzle.

Brine wasn't sure how long they sat in the library, poring over Kaya's notes. She lost track of time as she read, and she read everything—some of it twice. This couldn't be true. She wanted it not to be true. Kaya wasn't trying to cure the children: He had done this to them.

But Kaya was her father, and he was trying to save the island.

Yes, but he was taking children and draining their minds of everything.

And the one thought that turned everything inside her into a storm: She had also lost her memories. Had Kaya used her, too?

"Maybe it's not as bad as it seems," said Tom, his face crumpling.

"You think? Because, from where I'm sitting, this is very, very bad." She pushed the book off her lap. "You know when Cassie says things could be worse? This is what she means—this is the worst thing."

She started placing the books and papers back into the opening beneath the floor. Her whole body felt numb. "We have to find Peter." She wasn't sure what difference Peter would make, but she usually felt better when he was in trouble with her. She made sure the rug was back in place and everything looked the same as before. Then she opened the door and walked out and straight into Kaya.

CHAPTER 24

Orion's Keep, like the *Onion*, is full of magic, and its walls have not corroded. Stone would probably last longer than wood, but after all this time there should be some sign of damage. Three things, then, should have corroded but have not—the *Onion*, the castle, and Peter.

(from THOMAS GIRLING'S BOOK OF PIRATING ADVENTURE)

Boswell flattened himself to the ground and hissed.

Peter looked up at Marfak West. The ghost looked more transparent than usual, faded around the edges. "Not you again," groaned Peter. "I thought you couldn't leave the *Onion*."

"Who says I can't? It seems I can follow you around just fine. Isn't this fun? How is Kaya, by the way? I did tell him I'd come back, though I have to admit I didn't expect to do it like this."

Boswell blew fire at the ghost. It went straight through.

"Is Kaya really Brine's father?" asked Peter.

"That's not your story to know."

"Suit yourself." Peter turned his back on him. Of course,

that meant he had nothing to look at except the reptiles circling in the swamp, but he reckoned it was better than staring at the ghost's grinning face.

Marfak West drifted in front of him. "It's rude to ignore someone, you know." He sketched a shape in the air, paused, and did it again.

Peter sighed. "All right, what are you doing?"

"Showing you the spellshape for translocation," said Marfak West. "That's moving from one place to another with magic. It's a dangerous spell, because if you get it slightly wrong, you might translocate yourself to multiple places at once and end up looking like something Trudi cooked. It may, however, be preferable to being eaten by a crocosaurus."

"Is that what those things are?" Oddly, the presence of a dead, evil magician made the monsters seem less terrifying.

The crocosauruses swam closer. Boswell flapped into the water and blew a flame at one, and it backed away. How much fire did a dragon have, anyway? Peter wondered. He watched Marfak West repeat the spellshape. "I don't suppose you have any starshell?" he asked.

"As you keep pointing out, I'm a ghost. How am I supposed to carry starshell? In my ghost pockets?" Marfak West crossed his arms and smiled. "If you don't have starshell, it's a waste of time showing you the spellshape. I'll see you back on the *Onion*—if you make it back alive, that is. Otherwise I'll see you much sooner, I suppose."

He started to fade.

"Wait," said Peter.

The ghost disappeared with a faint, mocking laugh.

Boswell landed back beside Peter.

"Don't worry," said Peter, scratching the small dragon behind its scaly ears. "He's gone."

But if Boswell could see Marfak West, that meant the ghost was real, not a dream or hallucination. And if Marfak West was real, the spellshape was probably real, too. Marfak West wouldn't lie about magic. Not that it was going to do Peter any good if he didn't have starshell.

Then something that Hiri had said came into Peter's mind. Some spellstones work in pairs—like speakstones and movestones—and you move yourself between them.

Kaya had sent Peter here, so there must be a spellstone here somewhere. So all he had to do was find the other spellstone, and he could activate the spell to get back to the castle.

Peter spread his hands, trying to catch the prickling sensation of magic. He couldn't feel a thing, but that didn't mean anything—spellstones twisted magic around so that it was hard to feel.

"Keep guard, Boswell," said Peter. He began digging into the soft ground with his hands, pulling up soggy earth. If there was starshell here, the only place it would be safe was underground.

Boswell watched him for a while, then spread his wings, blew fire at the circling lizards, and took off across the swamp.

Peter jumped up. "Boswell!"

The little dragon didn't stop. Soon he disappeared into the darkness. Peter flopped back down onto the ground. Maybe he should try scratching Brine a message here so that if anyone ever found his body, they'd know he'd tried to escape.

Something stamped and crashed in the distance. A crocosaurus poked its nose out of the swamp and snapped at Peter curiously. Peter hurled a stone at it. "Get back!"

To his surprise, it worked. The crocosaurus fled—and not just that one, but all of them. They streaked away, disappearing under the water as they went.

Peter straightened up, watching the trees. The crashing and stamping increased in volume, and then several trees split apart and the biggest dinosaur Peter had ever seen in his life stepped through.

He couldn't see it clearly in the dark, which was just as well because he'd probably have run screaming into the swamp and drowned. A long neck, an even longer tail, and a body so vast, it eclipsed everything.

Everything, that is, apart from a small dragon-shaped object flying in front of it.

Boswell flew around the dinosaur's head, occasionally blowing out a stream of fire as if pointing out the way he wanted it to go. Astonishingly, the animal obeyed, lumbering into the swamp. The dark water sloshed around its body, and crocosauruses fled out of the way as it came.

The dinosaur reached the ground where Peter stood and stopped. Boswell flew down and nudged at Peter's legs.

"You want me to get on that thing?" asked Peter, feeling almost delirious with shock. Another part of his brain seemed to answer. *Boswell seems to have it under control. Can it be any more dangerous than staying here?*

The dinosaur lowered its head, and Peter climbed up and slid down to sit in the curve at the base of its neck. Its skin was surprisingly smooth and warm, like old leather that had been left out in the sun. Peter's arms just about met when wrapped around the creature's neck. He clung on tightly, grinning to himself and wishing there was someone besides Boswell to see him. He bet even Cassie had never done anything like this.

The dinosaur waded back through the swamp and paused on the far bank. Boswell flew in front, blowing out flames, and Peter sat back to enjoy the ride. Trees bent in front of him as the dinosaur marched through. He patted the animal on the neck, though it probably had as much effect as a butterfly hitting it.

There was nothing to do except cling on and hope for the best. In the end, the slow lurching lulled Peter half asleep and he lay back, cradled in the dip of the dinosaur's neck, trusting Boswell to lead them to safety.

And finally, a long while later, he heard people shouting.

▶┉┼┼╫●

Kaya knew, thought Brine. She could tell by the way he looked at them. He knew what they'd found in the library, and he was trying to decide what to do about it. For a moment she considered feigning innocence, but what would be the point?

"How could you?" she asked.

Kaya was still for so long that Brine thought he wasn't going to answer, but then he let out a long, quiet sigh and shook his head. "It wasn't my idea. The castle needs magic constantly just to exist, and the amount it needs is increasing every year. I told you about the magician, the one you call Marfak West. He had a theory that magic is a special form of energy. Anytime you change one kind of energy into another, some of it becomes magic. And so, he said, you should be able to deliberately—to change nonmagical energy straight into magic. And then, of course, we fought, and he killed most of us. But, later, I couldn't stop thinking about what he'd said. If I could find a way of turning other energy into magic, it would solve all our problems."

"Except that, when you take someone's creative energy, you take all their memories with it," said Brine. She had a bitter taste in her mouth. She should have known that Marfak West had started all this. "So my mother wasn't just trying to get me away from the castle—she was getting me away from *you*."

Kaya leaned on his staff, looking exhausted. "You were always telling stories; you created whole worlds in your mind.

All I did was take that potential and turn it into magic. You didn't know it, but you were saving the castle all by yourself. But then your mother stole you away from me. I haven't found another child like you, though I keep looking."

"But now you know what it does to people," said Brine. "Ren and the others. You're stealing their memories . . . their *lives*—don't you care?"

"Of course I care. But if Marfak erupts, everybody will die. What choice do I have?" Something in his face looked broken. "Please try to understand. Orion's Keep exists to save the island, and without magic and magi, the castle will fall and the whole island will be engulfed in boiling rock. I can't let that happen." He coughed. "Please go to bed now. We'll talk about this tomorrow."

"No," said Brine. How could Kaya have kept all this hidden from her, and what else was he hiding? "Where's Peter?" she demanded.

"Isn't he in his room?" Kaya answered too quickly, and avoided her gaze.

Brine turned cold. "You know he's not, don't you? What have you done with him?"

"What makes you think *I've* done anything with him? I'll take you back to your room. You'll feel better in the morning."

His staff began to glow. Brine stumbled back, her heart suddenly pounding so fast, it made her dizzy. She didn't know where the fear had come from; she knew only that it was threatening to swallow her whole.

Tom grabbed her hand and ran. They tore up the stairs and burst out onto the battlements. There, they had to stop. There was nowhere else they could go.

Chapter 25

GRILLED DINOSAUR FEET

One dinosaur foot per person, depending on size of dinosaur. Use the rest of the dinosaur to make pies or doughnuts. Wrap the feet in leaves and grill over a slow fire for an hour or more until cooked through. Season with seawater and curry powder.

Note—due to the size and speed of dinosaurs, this recipe hasn't yet been tested.

(from COOKING UP A STORME—
THE RECIPES OF A GOURMET PIRATE)

There was probably some sort of battle cry for this situation, Peter thought. The situation being the sight of Trudi, Bill, Rob, and Stella all clinging to the tops of trees while two very angry dinosaurs rampaged about on the ground, trying to get to them. They were quite big dinosaurs—each one the size of a large rowing boat, if you can imagine a boat with teeth and claws. But the dinosaur Peter rode was as large as a ship.

"Avast!" shouted Peter. His dinosaur squealed in terror and tried to run away, but it was so big that its tail swept through several trees on the way around and knocked one of the smaller dinosaurs headfirst into a pile of mud.

Stella's tree started to bend and crack. She yelled, and Peter urged his dinosaur forward. Stella landed on top of him. He untangled himself just in time to see the two smaller dinosaurs run at him, but Boswell swooped down and blew a torrent of flame right in their faces. They let out twin roars of surprise, and bolted.

"Peter!" shouted Trudi. She slid down from the tree. "Boswell flew away and . . . I see you've found him. How are you doing a disguisosaurus spell without magic?"

"It's not a disguise," said Peter, sliding down off the dinosaur. Boswell landed on Trudi's shoulder and started chewing her sleeve.

"Spider legs," she explained, tearing open a grease-soaked bag and offering the contents to the dragon. "You lot didn't like them, but Boswell has *discernment*."

He'd also gotten bits of spider stuck to his nose. The dragon licked them off and sneezed.

Trudi held out Peter's starshell. "We brought this, too. We thought it'd help find Boswell, and it worked, sort of."

Peter could have hugged her. Trudi seemed to guess what he was thinking and backed away hurriedly. "I suppose we should return to the *Onion* now."

"No," Peter replied. He cradled the box of starshell, letting the warmth of magic wash into his hands, and looked up into the sky. Tom and Brine were still up there, and they had no idea what was going on. He had to reach them. "Stand close to me," he said.

If you get the spellshape slightly wrong, you might translocate yourself to multiple places at once, Marfak West had said. But Peter wasn't going to get it wrong. He didn't even need to draw the spellshape. He didn't have to do anything except think about how desperately they all needed to get back to the castle. The magic did the rest. It poured out of the box around them, turning the forest amber, and then the night closed back in around the space where five people and one dragon had been standing.

I t took a few seconds for Peter to adjust to the fact that they were back on the castle and all of them in the right number of pieces. For those seconds it seemed that the whole world was shouting. Brine and Tom were yelling, Hiri and Ebeko running up the steps and shouting back, while Kaya stood in the middle of it all, both hands gripped around his staff. Kaya was the only one who was silent.

Peter stepped forward and Kaya saw him, then the magus's gaze fell on Boswell, who was still draped around Stella's shoulders, and he froze.

"That's a dragon."

"You're not the only magician who has them," said Peter, enjoying the magician's surprise. Then Brine grabbed him.

"Peter, what happened? We found Kaya's notebooks in

the library—well, Tom did. He's been experimenting on people."

"Tom's been experimenting on people?"

"No, stupid. Kaya." Her words washed over Peter in a flood. Magic coiled around his hands and flared away like the Stella Borealis.

It wouldn't take much to start another fight—but they'd already started several fights on this island, and none of them had done anyone any good. Peter drew in a steady breath and released the magic from his hands.

"Kaya is keeping dragon eggs," he said. His voice shook a little. "Four of them, at the bottom of the castle. I wondered how this castle could stay in the sky—that's how. He's using their magic."

He saw the confusion on Hiri's and Ebeko's faces. They hadn't known. It made Peter feel slightly better that they'd believed Kaya's lies as well.

Kaya slumped down over his staff. He looked very old all of a sudden, and very tired. "Yes, there are eggs. The secret has been handed down, First Magus to First Magus. The last remaining dragon eggs, kept safe while their magic keeps Marfak's Peak from erupting."

"But their magic isn't enough anymore, is it?" said Tom. "Magic is increasing in the world, but not as fast as you're using it. So you took it from people—the special magic that makes someone who they are. Brine first, and when she escaped, you used Ren and the other children."

At least Kaya didn't make excuses. The magus faced Brine squarely, not flinching from her furious gaze.

"It was my decision alone," he said, "so don't blame the others. Think what will happen if Marfak erupts. The whole island destroyed—every animal, every plant, every person. It's a case of trading one small evil to prevent a much bigger one."

Peter thought about it. Then he thought about the four dragon eggs, and about Brine, everything inside her slowly drained away to feed the castle's need for magic. "Evil doesn't come in sizes," he said. "You don't get small evils and big evil, like they're fish or apples. Bad is just bad."

"Really?" asked Kaya. "It seems to me that you're willing to sacrifice this whole island for the sake of four unhatched dragons." He shook his head wearily. "Sometimes we have to make the best of bad choices. I don't like what I'm doing here any more than you do, but the castle must not fail."

"Then we have a problem," said Cassie, stepping out from the doorway behind him. "Because letting you continue is the one thing we cannot do."

CHAPTER 26

According to not-quite-reliable sources (pirates), when you're stuck in sinksand, you should stand perfectly still because any movement will make you sink faster. The problem is, though, that standing still will make you sink anyway. Just a bit slower. If you're stuck, it's always better to try something than to do nothing.

(from BRINE SEABORNE'S BOOK OF PLANS)

The meeting the next morning must have been the first of its kind on the island. The three magi sat on one side of the long table in the castle hall. Stella and Cerro stayed close together, Cerro's broken legs stretched out on a stool. The fact that he was inside the castle seemed to bother him far more than the splints. Brine tried not to stare at Cassie and Ewan, who were standing on either side of the door, but she couldn't help noticing how Cassie kept her right hand on her sword hilt. Not threatening, not exactly: just reminding everyone it was there.

Boswell squirmed in Brine's lap, trying to get across her

to Peter. It was strange how quickly people had adjusted to the presence of a dragon. Last night the magi couldn't stop staring, but today, apart from an occasional glance, they treated him as if he'd always been here.

This meeting was getting them nowhere, she thought. Everyone had been talking for hours already. Shouting, mostly. Cassie had threatened to take the eggs by force, and Kaya had promised he'd kill the first pirate who tried.

Tom leaned toward Brine. "I know a story about a ship caught between a whirlpool and a great sea-monster. If the ship turned to the left, it would be crushed, and if it turned to the right, it'd be eaten."

Brine knew exactly how the ship felt, if ships could feel anything—trapped. "What happened to it?"

"I don't know," said Tom. He pushed his glasses back up his nose and threw a glance around the room. "The ship's crew thought they only had two choices—left or right—but if it was up to me, I'd lure the monster into the whirlpool."

Kaya frowned. "We've tried everything."

"No, you haven't," said Brine angrily. "You're doing what you've always done. You think the castle has to be saved and Marfak mustn't erupt, whatever the cost. But what if that's not true? What if you can make the volcano erupt and save the island, too? Then you won't need the castle anymore."

Kaya sighed and rested his forehead on his hands. "We can't save the island if Marfak erupts. That's the whole point. I know this situation isn't perfect . . ."

"Not perfect?" Brine jumped to her feet angrily, spilling Boswell onto Peter's lap. "Dragon eggs lying unhatched when the world needs them, children losing their minds. It's a lot worse than not perfect."

"I thought we were going to discuss this calmly," said Kaya.

"I am calm!"

Tom pulled her back into her seat. "Actually," he said, "Marfak is going to erupt whatever you do. Haven't you noticed the loose stones in the castle? This place is starting to fall apart." He spread his notebook on the table. "By my calculations, you have a month or two at most before bits start dropping off."

"He's right," said Peter. "The volcano has been dormant—but it's going to erupt again. If you really want to save the island, you have to do something now."

"And you think we should force an eruption?" Kaya rose from his chair. "It won't work. All our magic is tied up in spellstones."

"Not all of it," said Peter calmly. "You're drawing magic out of the eggs to feed your spellstones, but if you take the eggs away from the castle, their magic will be free. Marfak West was going to use one egg to blow up an entire island. We have four eggs and just one volcano. We can blow a hole in the side so big that the inside of the volcano will pour straight out into the sea. And then, when the island is safe, we'll hatch the eggs."

"Wild magic," said Kaya. He sat down slowly. "You still don't understand, do you? The moment the eggs leave the castle, the spellstones holding everything together will begin to fail. Orion's Keep will fall, and when the castle falls the island will be destroyed. Use your own magic to blow a hole in Marfak's side if you must, but you cannot take the eggs."

"I'm not powerful enough," said Peter. "Even if I took every piece of starshell here, I'd barely make a dent. But with the eggs, I can do it."

Brine's heart raced. Was this even possible? It had to be when the alternatives were to do nothing or to fight Kaya for the eggs. "Peter can do it," she said. She leaned half across the table, willing Kaya to listen. "Once Marfak's Peak has erupted safely, you won't need the castle. It doesn't matter if it falls."

"And if you fail?" asked Kaya. He fixed his gaze on Peter, his eyes bright with rage. "You just want the eggs for yourself. You're no different from your friend Marfak West. You think you can come here and take everything we have." He wheezed for breath. "I won't allow it."

Brine slumped back. This was useless—they'd never persuade him. Magic corroded, and Kaya had spent his whole life with more magic than Brine could imagine. Maybe he'd started off meaning well, but now his whole mind was fixed on the notion of preserving the castle, no matter the cost. Even if Marfak's Peak wasn't a threat, Kaya would want to keep the eggs, just in case. And then there'd be another crisis, and another.

Peter saw it, too, and his mouth set with his own variety of stubbornness.

"You see how impossible this is?" said Kaya. "Even if I gave you the eggs, what would you do? Climb halfway up Marfak's slope with the eggs and hope to magic yourself away before you drown in lava?"

"No," said Stella. "We'll use the balloon. I can fly Peter right across Marfak's Peak."

Peter grinned. The three magi stared at Stella in astonishment.

Cerro shifted position and scowled. "I never thought I'd find myself agreeing with a magus, but no. This is madness."

"Blowing up a volcano using dragon eggs and a balloon is actually quite sane by our standards," commented Cassie, studying her fingernails.

Brine's head was beginning to ache. Kaya could have tried to find a way to save the island and hatch the dragons years ago. Instead, he'd kept things exactly the same. He was like a man caught in sinksand, not moving in case it made him sink faster. And now it was up to the rest of them to pull him out of this mess. He was her father, she reminded herself. This was her home.

Kaya stood up and reached for his staff. "You are not taking the eggs."

"You say that as if you think you've got any choice," said Cassie. She stepped away from the wall, her smile bright. "We *are* taking the eggs. Your only choice is how painful you want this to be."

Hiri and Ebeko both jumped up. Ewan drew his sword. Kaya's staff flared with magical light.

"Stop!" shouted Brine.

Kaya was going to get himself killed. He couldn't beat Cassie, but he'd die rather than hand over the eggs. Unless they offered him something he wanted more—but what could he possibly want more than dragon eggs?

The answer scorched across her mind. It was her. His daughter. She'd saved the castle all by herself, at the cost of her memories. The dragon eggs absorbed magic, but she created it.

Brine stepped away from Tom and Peter. "What if you had another source of magic?" she asked. Her throat felt painfully tight all of a sudden, making it hard to get the words out. "You said you never found another child like me—so what if you had me again? Give us the dragon eggs and I'll stay here. If we succeed, then you won't need Orion's Keep anymore, and it can safely fall. But if we fail, you can use me to create the magic you need. That should keep the castle aloft for a while longer—long enough for you to make other plans."

Tom's face turned pale. "Brine, you can't! You'll lose your memory again."

"I know," she said, "but it's the right thing to do. Anyway, it won't happen, because we won't fail."

It felt like someone had hit her in the stomach as she said those words. She saw Cassie and Ewan start forward, and Kaya staring at her in openmouthed astonishment. Now she was between a whirlpool and a monster. She could spend the rest of her life here and never see the *Onion* again, or she could let Kaya drain all her memories—those were her only choices. But Kaya was her only family, and it was right to make sacrifices for family, wasn't it? Especially if it was the only way to stop a war between the pirates and the magi. And it might not be so bad living here with Boswell and the new dragons to look after.

She faced Kaya. "Everything changes," she said. "You can't fight it, any more than you can change the tide. Sometimes you just have to accept that and do the best you can."

Kaya had the look of an animal backed into a corner; his gaze flicked between Brine and the pirates. "This could kill you," he said. "I took your memories once. I won't do it again."

A small flame of warmth lit inside Brine. She'd worried that Kaya had only wanted her for her magic, but he really did care about her, she thought. "Peter won't fail," she said. "Marfak will erupt out to sea, and we'll hatch the dragon eggs and make a new home for ourselves in the village."

"A new home," echoed Kaya, his voice harsh. Then, as if he finally accepted he really had no choice, he let go of his staff and gave her a strange, frightened smile. "Very well," he said. "We'll try it."

"I haven't agreed to anything yet," snapped Cerro. "I came here for my son. I'm taking the children back to the village, and you won't stop me."

"You can have them," said Kaya. "And these." He set two starshells on the table. "Healstones."

He must have had them waiting all along, Brine thought. He'd planned to give them to Cerro, whatever happened. That was something good, wasn't it? She needed something good to fill the great hole that had suddenly opened up inside her.

Cerro picked up the stones and turned them over in his hands. "Stella, do you really think this plan will work?"

Stella nodded. "If Peter can handle the magic, I can handle the balloon."

Cerro let out a breath. "You'll fly from here to the seaward side of Marfak's Peak, and as soon as Peter has cast his spells you'll land safely. If you get into trouble, you'll abandon the plan straightaway. I don't want you taking any risks."

Brine wasn't sure it would be that straightforward, but Stella's face lit up. "I'll be careful, I promise." She reached out to stroke Boswell's scales. The little dragon squirmed and blew fire into Peter's lap.

"What about Marapi?" asked Stella over Peter's yelp of pain. "If Marfak is going to erupt, shouldn't we warn her?"

Cerro raised one shoulder. "Why? She won't leave the village, and she'll blame us for everything."

"On the other hand, she is your sister," Cassie pointed out. "And when this is over, you're going to have to live with her."

Cerro glowered at the table, then nodded. "I'll speak to her."

Cassie gave him her sunniest smile. "Good, then it's all

decided. Peter will take you back to the village with all the children. You should get everyone to the coast, as far from Marfak's Peak as you can. That way, if things go wrong, you'll still have a chance."

She didn't look at Brine, thank goodness, because Brine wasn't sure she could answer if anyone spoke to her. Cassie's voice seemed to come from the other side of the world.

"We're not leaving you here," said Peter in her ear. "We'll blow the volcano and hatch the eggs and then you can tell Kaya you're not staying. Cassie won't let you stay."

"Cassie won't have any choice," Brine muttered. She'd made Kaya a promise, and she couldn't go back on that. When this was over, the *Onion* would sail away and Brine would stay here. Never sail on the open sea again, never hear Ewan Hughes singing when he thought no one was listening or suffer Trudi's recipe experiments. Never argue with Peter or laugh with Tom.

Boswell butted into her from behind. She bent to pick him up and buried her face in his scales, feeling her tears trickle down over him. She wasn't doing this for Kaya, she thought: She was doing it for Boswell and for the four dragons yet unhatched. She'd be saving the dragons, and losing everything else.

Possibly even her mind.

CHAPTER 27

Reality turns into stories all the time. There are stories about Orion the mariner and Orion the dragon. Stories about Cassie O'Pia and the *Onion*. Can it work the other way around? Can a story gain so much life, so much magic, that it becomes real?

(from THOMAS GIRLING'S BOOK OF
PIRATING ADVENTURES)

The usual excitement Peter felt when using magic was missing as he prepared to take Cerro, Stella, and the group of children to the village. Brine was leaving the *Onion*. It was all he could think of.

Then do something about it, Marfak West's voice rang in his mind. *You're the magician: You think of something.*

Peter wished he could. He'd stay here with Brine, of course, and keep her safe from Kaya. It was an odd thing, though—he'd thought of leaving the *Onion* before, but he'd never realized how much he would miss the ship and her crew.

"Are you just going to stand there?" asked Stella. The

children were gathered around her, staring blankly into space. Cerro waited behind, leaning on his crutches. Once Kaya had explained how the healstones would make him sleep, Cerro had refused to use them until he knew everyone was safe.

Peter pulled his thoughts away from the *Onion*. One thing at a time, he reminded himself. First save the eggs, then the island, and then Brine.

He drew magic into his hand and let it spread out around them all. The castle blurred and vanished, and the next moment they were standing in the middle of the village. Marapi was bearing down on them, her face twisted with fury.

"We're back," said Cerro. "Before you start screeching, we need to talk."

Peter quietly magicked himself back to the castle. Cerro and Marapi would have to sort things out between themselves, he thought.

Given the chance, he'd have found somewhere quiet to sit, but Tom was waiting for him on the castle battlements and Peter had to appear pleased to see him even though he felt like he had a rock in his stomach.

"Where's Brine?" he asked.

Tom looked like he had swallowed several rocks himself. "With Kaya. And Cassie and Ewan are making plans, so I thought I'd come out here. Boswell needed some air." He pointed to where the little dragon was bounding about excitedly, taking off into the air every time they heard a teradon call.

"Why isn't he taking magic from the castle?" Tom asked.

"He probably is. It doesn't really matter now."

Peter watched as the dragon soared into the sky. He was outgrowing them, Peter thought, and it was a good thing, even though it hurt to think about it.

Tom hunched into his library robe. "Do you really think we can do this? Save the island and hatch the eggs?"

"We have to," Peter replied.

If they failed, Orion's Keep would be the only thing standing between the island and several tons of molten rock. And without the dragon eggs, the only source of magic was Brine.

"We'll do it," said Peter, more firmly. "And then, when the *Onion* leaves, Brine and I will stay and look after the new dragons."

He didn't ask Tom if he'd stay, too, because he knew Tom wouldn't.

Tom was a bit like the messenger gulls at Barnard's Reach—caged up in the library, all he'd wanted was to escape into the world, but now that he was flying free, part of him would always want to return home.

Tom took off his glasses and polished them furiously. "Let's not think about later. Anything could happen."

Then Peter saw Brine and his heart jumped. She'd changed out of her usual sailor clothes and was wearing a dress. Kaya must have found it for her. It was a mix of faded yellow and blue stripes, and the long skirt seemed to be mostly lace and holes.

Peter stood up quickly. "You look, um . . ."

"I look stupid," she said. She tried to smile, but her lips trembled. "Kaya said I ought to dress like a lady. Even Cassie doesn't wear this much lace." She tugged awkwardly at the skirt. "You can tell me I'm wrong if you like."

Peter shook his head. "No, you're right. Even Cassie doesn't wear that much lace."

She punched him.

"You know what I mean. I made him a promise. I can't just go breaking promises. Anyway, this *is* my home." She heaved a sigh. "I'm sorry."

"I'm not." Peter pulled his face into a grin even though it felt like something was breaking inside. "You got me into all this, and I wouldn't have missed it for the world."

"Oshima," Kaya called from the doorway. "I need you."

Brine sighed. "I'd better go see what he wants. Can we talk later?"

"Of course," said Peter. It already felt like there was a distance between them. He sat back down and wrapped his arms around his knees. After a while, Boswell flapped down and set fire to his shoes. Tom halfheartedly patted out the flames.

Cassie put her head out of a door. "What are you two talking about?"

"Nothing much," said Peter. "When are we going to do this?"

She thought for a moment. "At sunrise. Dawn is the traditional time of day for death-defying adventure."

CHAPTER 28

Though dread Marfak's Peak is preparing to wreak
Destruction most awful and dire,
Yet never you fear, for Cassie O'Pia
Will save you from lava and fire.

(from THE BALLAD OF CASSIE O'PIA,
Verse 317, Author Unknown)

The sky was only just turning light. Stella's balloon tugged impatiently at the ropes mooring it against the castle battlements. Brine stood and watched it while Peter, Tom, and Stella swapped stories around her. They were trying to cheer her up, Brine thought, and she wished they wouldn't. She didn't feel like being cheered up right now. Even the sight of Boswell setting fire to Peter didn't help.

"Cerro and Marapi had the most tremendous row yesterday," said Stella. "Cerro wanted to take everyone to the coast and Marapi wouldn't listen. You'd think it was Cerro's fault that Marfak is going to erupt. They yelled at each other for ages, and then Cerro said he was going to the coast and people could either come with him or stay with Marapi. So now the village is split. About a quarter of them left."

Brine had been secretly hoping that everyone would have gone with Cerro. "How is your brother?" she asked. "Are the children getting their memories back now that they're out of the castle?"

"Not yet. Cerro tried using the healstones on Ren, and they did nothing. He still won't use them on his legs. He said he'll sleep when the island is safe, or when he's dead—whichever comes first. This is so typical of my father—he rushes into things without thinking, and half the time he causes more trouble than he solves."

"He's just like Cassie, you mean," said Brine, and for a moment she was able to smile. "Cassie tried to sell me and Peter once because she thought we'd be better off living on a rich island than on the *Onion*. And then she went sailing off to Magical North because her worst enemy dared her to."

"And she took me off Barnard's Reach because Brine told her to," said Tom.

Stella laughed. "Maybe Dad and Cassie should get together?"

"Not going to happen," Ewan Hughes interrupted.

"But—" Stella fell silent.

Ewan gave them all a stare that lasted half a minute, then nodded as if he'd just won the argument and stamped away.

Stella gazed after him. "Is he in love with Cassie?"

Brine had never even thought about it. Now that she did, she noticed how Ewan was never more than two steps away from Cassie, always watching her in case she needed him.

Peter shook his head and laughed. "Cassie's only in love with the *Onion*."

Brine supposed he was right. She knew how Cassie felt because she loved the *Onion*, too, and every time she remembered that she was never going to see the ship again, it felt like a sword had gone through her.

Don't think, she reminded herself. *Or, at least think about the stories if the plan succeeds.* Because if she thought about what would happen to her if the plan didn't work, she would be tempted to give up now.

Just then, Kaya, Hiri, and Ebeko came onto the battlements. Kaya carried the four dragon eggs in a basket of sand, and he wore an expression Brine had never seen before. The deep lines of tiredness around his eyes and mouth had gone. When he caught Brine's gaze, he smiled. He looked almost free, she thought with surprise.

Boswell went mad, roaring and blowing flames, turning frantic somersaults in the air until Peter caught him.

"How long until the castle begins to fall?" he asked.

Kaya laughed. "I have no idea. I've never done this before. An hour at most, I'd guess. Hiri and Ebeko will take everyone down to the island. Brine and I will stay here until the end, in case we need to maintain the castle."

Cassie strolled out behind him. "One hour until everything

falls apart or blows up," she said. "It could be worse. Ewan and I will stay here with you, in case you need help."

Her gaze hardened as she looked at Kaya, and Brine recognized the silent message. *Betray us*, it said, *and you will be sorrier than you can possibly imagine.*

Brine didn't know whether Kaya got the message, but he said nothing. Turning away from Cassie, he gestured to Hiri and Ebeko, and the three of them walked away, joining the group of castle guards and servants who were gathering on the battlements. A staff flared with magic and two people vanished.

"Tom," called Hiri. "Your turn."

Tom stepped back. "I'll wait until Brine leaves."

Brine squeezed his hand, grateful to him for staying, though wishing the magi would hurry up so they could get this over with.

Stella swung herself into the basket, and Peter handed her the dragon eggs. Then Peter hugged Brine quickly. "See you on the ground."

He climbed into the basket and Stella cut through the rope that strained from balloon to battlement.

The balloon began to rise at once. Boswell shrieked and flapped after them.

"Send him back!" shouted Brine.

"I can't. I'm sorry. We'll see you . . ." The rest of his words were lost as the balloon was swept away.

"Wait!" Brine cried, but her voice was swept away as well. Tears filled her eyes. "I was going to say good luck!"

"You can say well done when they're finished," said Cassie, gazing out after the balloon. "I guess now we wait and see what happens."

Kaya took Brine's hand. "I'm sorry," he said.

"Sorry about what?" asked Brine as the castle vanished around them.

The next moment, Brine found herself standing on the deck of the *Onion*.

CHAPTER 29

I must go into the sky again, though I don't want to go,
When all I have is a patched-up balloon and a basket hung below,
And the cold wind and the hot fire, and the mountain shaking,
And I cannot shift the constant dread that the ropes are breaking.
I must go into the sky again, though I fear this won't go well,
Sustained with hope of dragons and the stories we will tell.
And all I ask is a balloon that holds and keeps on flying,
And a weak spot on the mountainside and us not dying.
I must go into the sky again, above the rolling sea,
And all I ask is for dinosaurs to stay away from me.
And a low breeze and a calm flight and a victory splendid,
And a long sleep for a week at least when this is ended.

(from THE SKY'S THE LIMIT by Peter Magus)

The lurching basket had been bad enough before. Peter had been afraid he was going to die. This time, he was afraid he wouldn't and he'd have to live through the next hour in stomach-jolting misery.

He put his hand on the box of dragon eggs to keep it steady. Boswell's egg had been so cold, it had stripped the skin from his hands. These eggs were hot. The flecks of gold in the sand were starting to blur together and a coil of smoke rose.

"Better hurry," said Peter. Much longer and the eggs might burn through their bed of sand, through the box, through the basket, and send them all plummeting to the ground. He put his hands in his pockets, feeling the pieces of starshell there. He'd taken as many as he could carry, and his trousers would probably fall apart soon, which was a more embarrassing problem.

Marfak's Peak rushed up beneath them, a black cone spewing smoke into the sky while, high above, the castle teetered. The cloud it had rested on was already starting to thin. Cassie was with them, Peter reminded himself. Cassie would make sure everyone got out safely.

Then the balloon swung around, racing on until they were over the sea. Peter took a long look at the sapphire waves and the *Onion* waiting offshore. He wished he knew what was happening on board right now.

He moved back from the eggs as the heat coming off them was making him sweat, and he took a piece of starshell out of his pocket. "I'm going to cast a finding spell to look for a weak point on the volcano. Once you get us there, you'll need to hold the balloon as steady as you can while I hit the spot with magic. The force of the blast will throw us backward, and I don't want us to crash into the sea. Then once we're sure the volcano is erupting out to sea, we'll land the balloon and I'll hatch the eggs."

The balloon wobbled. Stella pulled on a rope and they steadied. "You really mean to hatch the eggs?"

"Of course. What else would I do?"

She shrugged and pushed her hair back. "Kaya would have kept them for himself. You saw his face, didn't you? He didn't want to give up that much magic. With those eggs, you'd be the most powerful magus alive."

"I don't want to be the most powerful magician alive; I want there to be dragons." The truth of it hit Peter and made him smile. *Take that, Marfak West,* he thought, *I'll never be like you.* "This will be easy," he said. "I'm not going to let Marfak erupt over the island. The dragons will need somewhere to live once they hatch."

"Do you care about anything apart from dragons?" asked Stella, smiling. "Come on, then. Let's do this. You see that rope by your head? Grab it and pull it toward me."

Having something to do helped. Peter followed Stella's instructions and avoided looking down. Every so often he caught sight of the *Onion,* still waiting, and the sight opened up an empty space inside him. He was saving the dragons only to leave them here with Brine. This island, with its mountains and forests, and its gold-filled sand for nesting, was exactly right for them.

Maybe it wouldn't be too bad living here. Cassie could

even come back to visit, and the island would have new stories to hear of the *Onion*'s adventures.

"Peter," said Stella.

Peter looked up and saw dark shapes coming toward them. Teradons.

CHAPTER 30

Necessity is the mother of invention, and the father of evil.
Sometimes, it is easier to do the kind thing or the good thing,
but we must always do what is necessary.

(from RECORDS OF ORION'S KEEP—
First Magus Belen Kaya)

Brine turned a slow circle, trying to believe what she was seeing. She was back on the *Onion*. Around the ship, the crew stood as still as statues while the castle servants and guards waited quietly. Hiri and Ebeko stood in the middle of the deck.

"What's going on?" asked Brine.

The air shimmered beside her and Kaya appeared. Brine swung around. "Kaya, what's happening? You said you couldn't send us straight to the *Onion*. You said you needed a move-stone at each end."

"We do have a movestone at each end," said Kaya. He walked across to Tim Burre, who was standing stiff and still, and took something out of the pirate's hand.

Ewan Hughes's voice came out of it, tiny and distorted. "Anyone? Can anyone hear me?"

"Ewan!" cried Brine. She started forward, but Kaya tossed the stone to Ebeko.

"The speakstone I sent back with your friends also had a movespell engraved into it," he said. "I thought I might need a way to get onto the ship, and it turned out I was right."

"But why are we even on the ship?" asked Brine. "We should be back at the castle. You need me there in case Peter fails." She reached out to take his hand, but Kaya drew back and then limped slowly away from her.

"I'm sorry," he said, not looking at her. "There's been a change of plan."

Brine felt a creeping chill up through her legs. Hiri stared down at the deck, his face ashamed, but Ebeko looked right at Brine and her face was filled with a spiteful triumph.

"Orion's Keep is finished," Ebeko said. "Your friends saw to that. They forced us into a corner. We had no choice. Did you really think we'd abandon the castle and everything in it so we could live quietly on the island, answering to Cerro or Marapi? Your friends took our castle; we're taking their ship."

Brine's eyes filled up with furious tears. "You can't do this! Kaya, please, Tom's still in the castle. He hasn't done anything to you. Are you really going to let him die?"

"If Peter's plan succeeds, he'll have plenty of time to go back for them," said Kaya. "And by then we'll be far away." His voice trembled; his eyes filled with an awful resolution. "Please try to understand. We can't captain the ship if the former captain is on board. Hiri and Ebeko have put the crew to sleep, but the spell will break soon. I'm going to explain there's been a terrible accident and we are the only survivors. I'll tell them we have to set sail straightaway or Marfak will erupt into the sea and kill us all. I need you to help me convince them. They'll listen to you."

The fire in Brine's throat turned into a volcano. When they had forced Kaya to give up the dragon eggs, they hadn't just pushed him into a corner, she thought; they'd pushed him off the edge of sanity. She backed away from him. He really believed she'd give in, just like that, and do what he said.

Kaya put a hand out and gently stroked a tear from her cheek. "I'm doing this for you, Oshima. I told you, I stole your memories once, and I won't do it again. I know you'd never be happy living on the island. I will captain the *Onion* for the time I have left and you'll help me. When I die, you'll take over from me. Trust me, it's better this way."

"Better? Better for Tom and Cassie and Ewan to die? Better for the crew to live as your slaves?" Brine threw herself at him, trying to wrestle the staff from his hand. Ebeko ran and pulled her off and held her around the waist as she kicked and struggled, and Kaya watched sadly. He looked sorry; that was the worst thing. As if he genuinely regretted what he was about to do, but he was going to go ahead and do it anyway.

"What would you prefer?" he asked sadly. "Tell the truth and set off a fight in which most of us will be killed, or accept the inevitable? Cassie will understand. Either Peter will go back for her in time or she'll get the heroic end she's always dreamed of. Maybe one day people will tell tales of her last heroic battle against the one enemy she couldn't defeat. Tragedy has a special appeal, you know. It makes a story get into your heart and stay there."

"No, it doesn't!" Brine shouted. "Tragedy just means people die."

The tip of Kaya's staff began to glow. "You still don't understand, do you?" he said. "You're young, and your memories of Orion's Keep are lost. We'll make new memories together—starting now. Remember your duty as my daughter."

Brine's thoughts swam. "What about my duty to my friends?"

The lines around his mouth grew hard. "Your friends are bravely sacrificing their lives at this very moment. You can't do anything about it, so you might as well just accept the fact. The sooner you do, the easier it'll be for you."

Brine felt her eyes begin to close. Maybe Kaya was right. She felt like she was a ship being swept along by the sea. She couldn't control the direction she was taking, but she could decide whether she sank or stayed afloat. Kaya was going to do this anyway, so she might as well make the best of it, stay afloat, do what he wanted. Besides, she was tired of fighting.

Then she heard a laugh, and her eyes snapped open.

Kaya nearly dropped his staff.

Mind control, Brine thought. Kaya's staff was full of spells, and of course one of them would be mind control. The First Magus had to control his people. Brine sagged back, resting her whole weight on Ebeko, and then she kicked back.

Ebeko let go of her with a startled yell. Brine kicked her again then ran, tearing past the frozen crew and through the open hatch to the underdeck. She heard Kaya's voice. "Don't worry—she can't go anywhere."

Brine slammed the hatch and locked it, then dropped down the steps. She stood, panting. She was trapped. All she could do was hide and hope the spell wore off the crew before Kaya found her. She ran past the hammocks and Trudi's galley and on into the place where Peter always hid, the small space between packing crates at the back of the ship. Some of the boxes from the castle were here, too. A few of them held books, but others were full of sand that glittered with flecks of gold. Of course, if the magi were going to steal the *Onion*, they'd want gold to fund their voyage.

Then something stirred beside her. A patch of cold that wasn't there a moment ago.

"I was wondering when you'd show up," said Marfak West.

CHAPTER 31

After the extinction of the dragons, the magi tried to re-create
them. They cast spells on various animals and birds on the
island, but instead of dragons, they created monsters, which
people called dinosaurs. These animals are persistent and
intelligent, and some of them can even be trained.

(from STORIES OF APCARON)

Peter watched the teradons soar closer. He wasn't too
worried—he'd seen Boswell chase off a whole flock of
them on the *Onion*, and he didn't expect these would be any
different. Most of them began circling as soon as they came
near the balloon, and Boswell soared out to meet them. But
one of them came straight for the balloon, its claws outstretched, and Peter saw the glint of gold around its leg. Peter
aimed a push spell at it. It veered aside, but the basket swung
wildly as well.

Stella grabbed hold of a rope. "They're Marapi's," she said.
"I don't believe this. She's trying to stop us."

Of course she was, Peter thought; they should have expected this. They were about to change the island forever, and Marapi wanted to keep everything the same. She wanted to stay in charge. Everyone said that magic corrupted, but it seemed that any type of power could corrode the mind until only the desire for more power remained.

He leaned out and watched the teradons. They were keeping well away from Boswell, but they weren't fleeing, either. Peter pushed at another pair, and the basket swung backward. Aldebran Boswell's third law of motion, he thought—for every action there was an opposite reaction. The balloon already felt unstable. He couldn't just keep hitting the teradons out of the way.

"Take us lower," said Peter. Boswell screamed at some nearby teradons and they scattered, but seconds later they came back, keeping their distance for now, but for how much longer?

Stella adjusted the heatstones, and the balloon sank lower in the sky. Boswell landed on the edge of the basket, making it swing even more. They had to finish this quickly, Peter thought. Leaning over the basket's edge, he saw a dull red crack running in a diagonal stripe about halfway up the volcano on the coastal edge of the island. "Aim for there," he told Stella. "Keep the balloon as steady as you can."

Stella nodded and tugged on one of the ropes, releasing a panel of fabric on the balloon. A gentle hiss of escaping air came from overhead and the balloon dropped sharply, making Peter's stomach lurch. At the same moment, a group of teradons plunged straight for them.

Peter swept up a handful of magic and drew a quick spellshape to push them all back. He managed to catch two of them, and they collided and spun away, shrieking in pain. Peter watched, feeling slightly ill. He didn't like hurting things with magic, he decided, and the knowledge made him glad. Whatever kind of magician he turned out to be, he was not going to be like Marfak West, who'd hurt people for fun.

The ground swung dizzyingly, not too far below. At this rate, they were going to fly straight into Marfak's Peak. Peter held on to the dragon eggs to keep them steady. Some saying about not putting all your eggs in one basket flashed through his mind. "We're too low now," he said worriedly. "Take us back up."

"I can't," said Stella. "The heatstones are running out."

Peter grabbed Boswell as he swooped past and pushed him under the balloon. The dragon struggled as teradons squawked, then he blew out a gust of orange flame that disappeared into the balloon's canopy. Peter grinned in triumph. "Now we have heat," he said.

The balloon billowed out and their descent slowed. Boswell seemed to understand what Peter wanted him to do and started breathing out fire in little gusts, enough to provide some lift without setting the balloon alight.

Then Peter heard a shriek behind and turned to see three

teradons diving together. He reacted without thinking, sweeping his hands around to bat the teradons aside, and sent the basket into a swinging spiral. The box of dragon eggs slid sideways, and so did Boswell.

"Peter, look out!" shouted Stella.

Peter swung around, too late to do anything. Boswell's next flaming breath set the box of eggs alight. For a second, the flames leaped high, and then, as if all the heat had been sucked out of the air, the fire went out.

There was a moment of shaky silence. Stella grabbed Boswell. "That was close."

Peter could only stand and stare. Stella didn't understand what had just happened. Dragon eggs needed two things to hatch—fire and magic—and now they had both. Back on Marfak West's ship, Boswell's egg had absorbed fire from all around it, sat dormant for a minute or so, and then it had exploded.

He looked at the eggs, all four of them, and then he looked up at the fragile canopy of the balloon. "Look after Boswell," he said.

He put one hand on the box of eggs, put his other on the starshell in his pocket, and thought about how he needed to get down to the mountainside, right next to that long crimson crack in the rock.

"Peter, what are you doing?" asked Stella.

Magic pooled in Peter's hand and flared to life, and the world shifted.

Another teradon shrieked, but the sound was suddenly far away. Peter was sure Stella must have shouted, too, but he didn't hear her at all. His feet hit solid rock, and he stumbled and almost fell. A sudden gust of smoke set him coughing. He'd cast the spell exactly right, setting himself down just a few steps away from the crack in the mountain.

Looking up, Peter saw the balloon dipping toward him and teradons still circling. He reckoned he had about a minute before the eggs started to hatch, and when they did, they'd draw in every scrap of magic from the area and then explode. The only thing Peter could do was to leave the eggs here and magic himself back to the balloon while he still had time. With a bit of luck, the explosive hatching would rupture the mountain. The dragons might survive, and he and Stella would have a chance to get away.

But "might survive" wasn't good enough—not after he'd come this far.

"This was a stupid plan right from the start," said Peter, dragging the box of eggs up to the scarlet crack in the volcano. He half hoped Marfak West would be listening, but there was no response from the magician's ghost. Fine. He didn't need Marfak West's help anyway. Peter pulled his sleeves down over his hands to protect them from the heat of the eggs, then he picked the first one up and placed it carefully on the ground. Smoke coiled around it, not all of it from the volcano.

If the four eggs hatched along the crack in the mountain, it might be enough to blow out the whole mountainside, but he couldn't leave the little dragons to die in the lava. If he waited, he might be able to grab each dragon as it hatched. He wasn't sure how he'd get away then, but he'd think of something.

The second egg trembled as he set it down.

If he survived this, Peter promised silently as he placed egg number three, he'd leave all the planning to Brine forever. Brine thought about things like teradons attacking just when everything was going well.

The fourth egg was so hot when he picked it up that his sleeve caught fire, but the flames vanished straight into the egg. Peter put it down where he was standing—there wasn't time for anything else—and scrambled back to crouch in the scrubby grass behind a rock. He wished he'd asked Tom how fast lava moved, but surely it couldn't be that fast. Rock was still rock, after all, even if it was hot, and rocks weren't known for their speed. He might still have time to grab the baby dragons as they hatched and run before Marfak erupted completely.

The first egg began to wobble, and then its shell blazed white as it burned with magic.

A rope hit the ground at Peter's feet.

"Peter!" yelled Stella. "Climb!"

He hadn't even noticed the balloon coming close; he'd been so intent on the dragon eggs. He jerked his head up and saw Stella hanging out of the basket right above him, so close that he could almost grab her hand.

He stood up and waved his arms at her. "Stella, there's no time. Go higher! Quickly—the eggs are hatching."

The first egg exploded.

Fire shot skyward in a roar as if the world had been torn in two. A rush of wind threw Peter backward. He landed flat on his back, the air knocked out of him. Above, he saw Boswell soaring up to safety, the circling teradons torn apart by the blast, and the balloon collapse in on itself and then come tumbling down.

CHAPTER 32

Never be last to leave any structure that is falling apart.
(from THOMAS GIRLING'S BOOK OF
PIRATING ADVENTURE)

Kaya's estimate of an hour had been optimistic: Orion's Keep was already starting to fall apart. Tom pulled a lump of stone off the battlements. Stone ought to be one of the most solid things in the world, yet it crumbled to nothing between his fingers. His vision swam as he looked over the side. He knew the castle hadn't risen in the sky, but the ground looked farther away than ever. He could just about see Stella's balloon, skimming rapidly around the slopes of Marfak.

"Tim? Trudi?" said Ewan into the speakstone. No one answered. "Useless thing," he said, hurling it over the side of the castle. "I knew we shouldn't have trusted that magician. Magicians are all the same."

"Apart from Peter," corrected Tom automatically. He saw

movement in the sky near the balloon, and his heart jumped. "Are those teradons?"

Ewan watched for a moment. "Don't worry about Peter," he said. "He'll be all right. We need to find a way out of here."

Tom didn't want to argue with Ewan, but Peter was about to fly into a volcano hanging from a balloon made of flammable material and with teradons chasing him. If Tom were making a list of things that were all right, that wouldn't even make it onto the page.

Tom tried to breathe steadily. His head felt funny. It was probably the height, or the fact that height wouldn't be a problem much longer. "Just because Kaya hasn't come back yet doesn't mean he won't," he said. "Brine won't let him leave us. There's probably just been some holdup."

"Our problem is a lack of holdup," said Ewan as one of the four corner towers started to collapse in on itself. "Is there another way out? Remember how we got trapped at Magical North and found a tunnel?"

Cassie cast a glance over the side of the castle, and her face turned greenish. "I think we've already established that there are no tunnels. Tom, do you still have that finding stone you were talking about?"

Of course. Tom got it out and rubbed it hard. "How do we get off this castle?" he said.

Amber magic speared out and headed directly down.

"That figures," said Ewan.

Cassie gave them a shaky smile. "It could be worse. Let's

assume we're on our own, then. We need rope, or something we can turn into rope. It's a long climb down, but we can do it."

"And Kaya will come back for us," said Tom determinedly. "Or Peter will."

"Yes. One of those two." She took a few unsteady steps toward the nearest door, then paused and straightened. Her hand crept up to grip the emerald around her neck. "I don't know about you," she said slowly, and some of the fire returned to her voice, "but I find that sitting around on disintegrating castles is exciting for a few minutes, but after that it gets really quite dull. Let's keep ourselves busy, shall we?"

They gathered ropes, sheets, anything that could be cut into strips and tied together. Tom gathered a couple of small books from the library. Many of the shelves were already empty, and Kaya's secret under-floor stash of books was gone, too.

"We're going to climb down, remember," said Cassie. "You won't be able to take anything with you."

Tom nodded as he stuffed the books into a bag. They'd never be able to tie all of this together into a rope, and as for climbing down, maybe Cassie and Ewan could do it, but he definitely couldn't.

But at least it gave them something to do while they waited to be rescued—because they would definitely be rescued. Tom kept hoping through all the long minutes during which Kaya failed to come back for them. Kaya was with Brine, and Brine wouldn't let him leave them here.

Then the air trembled, and a roar of fire and smoke tore Marfak's Peak in two. The seaward side of the volcano vanished under a fog of thick black smoke.

"Something's happening," said Ewan. He could have been commenting on the weather.

Tom nodded. That would be Peter, saving the dragons and the island. That was good. He'd probably guess they were still stuck on the castle, and Stella would bring the balloon back for them. They'd have to write the whole story down later so they could send it back to Barnard's Reach.

A piece of the castle battlements fell away, then another of the corner turrets crumbled and slid off into the sky. Tom tied knots faster. It would be all right, he promised himself. Peter would come back for them, or Brine would be back soon. Brine always came up with a plan; she wouldn't leave them here.

CHAPTER 33

Stories make us who we are. With all the millions of stories
in the world, the only one that really matters is your own.

(from THOMAS GIRLING'S BOOK OF
PIRATING ADVENTURE)

Brine wasn't in the mood for any more surprises. She folded
her arms across her chest and glared at the ghost of
Marfak West. "You're dead," she said. He'd better be, because
if he was still alive, it meant they were all in far more trouble
than she'd thought.

The ghost gave a little shrug. "Peter keeps telling me the
same thing, and yet I'm still here. Weird, isn't it? Don't worry,
I'm not going to kill you. The afterlife is quite tedious enough
without inviting you into it."

Brine unstuck her tongue from the roof of her mouth.
"I thought Peter imagined you."

The ghost laughed. "You should know better than that.
Peter may have hidden talents, but imagination isn't one of

them. My guess is that when Boswell's egg hatched, some part of me was baked into the shell. And when those pieces of shell regained their magic, I came back. As long as you have magic, you have me." He smiled. "The *Onion* and I are getting on very nicely. We've had some interesting conversations."

Brine put her hand on the wall to steady herself and felt a vague throbbing through her palm. "How can a ship have a conversation?"

"It can't," said Marfak West. "That's your mistake—you thought you were on board a ship. In your mind, this ship has always been the *Onion*, and so that's what it is for you. You forget that I sank the real *Onion* at Magical North."

Marfak West made even less sense when he was dead.

A thumping came from overhead: Kaya breaking through the hatch. Brine shrank back against the crates. "I haven't forgotten. This was Aldebran Boswell's ship the *Orion*. But it's the *Onion* now."

"It's actually far more complicated than that. Reality often is. The universe is changeable, and sometimes it doesn't make up its mind what to be until someone is looking."

"Boswell said that," said Brine.

"Boswell was a very clever man."

"Oshima?" Kaya's voice echoed in the dark underdeck. "Oshima, where are you? Hiding won't change anything, and we need to talk."

Brine pressed herself as far back into the gap as she could.

"I don't see why you're objecting so much," said Marfak

West. "This is what you've wanted, isn't it? To be captain of the *Onion*?"

Denial sprang to Brine's lips and died there. Marfak West smiled.

"Maybe you're right," said Brine. "But not like this. If I became captain now, with the crew under a spell, with Cassie and Tom and Ewan all dead, with Peter trapped on Marfak's Peak, this wouldn't be the *Onion* anymore."

The hatch crashed back, and footsteps sounded on the steps. "Oshima," said Kaya, "I am ordering you to come out."

Brine stayed where she was, waiting breathlessly.

A crate moved.

"There you are," said Kaya. He stopped, his eyes widening in shock.

"Surprised to see me?" asked Marfak West.

Kaya's staff began to glow. "You're dead. You don't belong here."

"That makes two of us," said Marfak West, "but you know the story. Marfak will rise and the island will die in flames." The shadows around him turned red, writhing like fire. Brine didn't know whether a ghost could actually hurt someone, and after everything Kaya had done, she didn't care, but still she stepped between the magus and the ghost.

"This isn't Kaya's fault," she said. "He only ever wanted to save the island. We pushed him into this. Besides, he's my father."

The flames around Marfak West died. The ghost stared

at Brine, then he threw back his head and laughed. "Your father? Is that what he told you?"

Brine's world stopped.

"Don't believe him," said Kaya. But the flash of guilt on his face had already given him away. Besides, Marfak West rarely lied. He used the truth as a weapon to hurt you, but he wasn't a liar—not like Kaya.

Brine put a hand on the wall to steady herself. Her chest ached as if she'd been holding her breath for days, and now she was gulping in air faster than she could cope with. "If Kaya isn't my father, who is?" She hadn't recognized anyone on the island until she'd seen Kaya.

Kaya tried to drag Brine away, but Marfak West moved far quicker. The ghost's fingers closed around the magus's wrist and passed through. Kaya screamed and jerked back.

"I helped raise you," he shouted, clutching his injured hand. "You were special from the start. I loved you like a daughter—even before I found out what you could do. Magic is potential, it is the ability to shape the world, and you had *so much* potential. You could tell a story and make it come true. You were the answer we were looking for. You still are."

His staff glowed brighter, and Brine felt the urge to believe him, to accept all this and just do as he wanted. She shook her head to clear it. He was trying to control her again, and it wasn't going to work. She pressed her fingers into the wall until they ached.

"Where are my parents?" she asked. She turned to Mar-fak West. "Did you kill them?"

"Why does everyone think I go round killing people? They were alive and well when I left the castle."

"Then what happened?" asked Brine.

Kaya didn't answer, but Brine didn't need him to, because, as if a final obstacle had slid aside in her mind and a box had opened, she remembered.

O shima."

    Oshima didn't remember the two people bent over her, or even that her name was Oshima. Her thoughts had been in tatters for so long. But the man and woman were urging her out of bed and then carrying her up the steps to the top of the castle, where the sky was jewel-bright with stars.

    For some reason, the man was carrying the magus's staff: Oshima recognized it.

    Then the castle vanished and they were running through trees to where a boat waited. They settled her in, and the woman hung a piece of bright shell around Oshima's neck. "For protec-tion," she said, and kissed her.

    The man opened a bag and took out more shells. He rubbed each one and they all began to glow. But the woman turned back to the shore with a cry as the air parted behind them and the magus appeared.

Then a sound louder than a dinosaur's roar, and the people were shouting and pushing at the boat. But their hands slipped away, and Oshima was alone.

After that, there was only a sea in bright sunlight and, later, people with strange white faces looking at her.

><><><><

Brine blinked a few times and stood trembling. It took her a moment to come back to herself and remember what she was doing here. Her parents' voices filled her mind. She could see their faces—quiet and serious and always looking slightly afraid. Now she knew why. "You killed them," she said. "They tried to escape with me, and you killed them."

"That's not true," said Kaya. His breath came in wheezes. "They cast a spell to send you away, and I couldn't stop them. You disappeared, and as the spell was starting to fail, they tried to follow. They must have known it was hopeless. Most of the spell's magic was already used up by sending you away. They could have ended up anywhere."

"But they did end up somewhere?" A surge of hope cut through the fear that gripped her. "They're still alive?"

"They might be," said Kaya. "I spent my time looking for you, not them." He coughed. "I'm sorry we lost them, but they broke Orion's Law; they knew how important you were. If I had had you these past three years, Orion's Keep would have had all the magic it needed."

Brine barely heard him. Her parents were alive; the thought filled her mind and she couldn't help but smile.

"You don't need them," said Kaya, frowning uncertainly at her. "I'm not your real father, but I will be like a father to you—the father you should have had all along. We'll travel together, learn from each other, and when I die, everything I have will be yours."

He reached out to her. His eyes were dark and shining and quite, quite mad.

Brine backed into the wall. Kaya really believed what he was saying. He'd convinced himself that he'd had no choice about what he'd done, that he'd done everything for the right reasons. He'd probably even come to believe she really was his daughter and wonder why she didn't love him back.

"You're too late," said Marfak West. "You can't control her. You can't control the ship, either; the *Onion* doesn't want you here. I told you once before, people who don't understand magic shouldn't use it."

"I know what magic is," snarled Kaya. "It is life; it is potential; it is change."

"Yes, and you want to lock it up inside stone walls until it stagnates and dies with age." The ghost stepped out into the open, and Brine found she could see straight through him. "You could have dealt with Marfak's Peak years ago, but you spent all your power on keeping things the same. You still don't understand—anything that won't change is dead already."

Kaya backed away. "You're the one who's dead. You don't belong here, and you will leave. As for this ship, I claim it as my own and it will obey me."

He slammed his staff down onto the deck—onto wooden boards filled to overflowing with a hundred years of magic. Magical power raced into his staff faster than the spellstones could cope with. The underdeck flooded with light as every spell in the staff came to life at once, and the spellstones fought to cast them all. Kaya cried out and collapsed to his knees. The air shimmered in twenty different places all around him, and Brine saw flashes of sea and mountain and trees through them.

Then Kaya vanished.

It happened as fast as drawing breath. One moment there, and then he was gone. His staff fell to the floor and rolled gently across to Brine's feet. In a daze, she bent and picked it up.

"Where did he go?" she asked.

The ghost of Marfak West studied his fingernails. "How many movestones did he have in that staff?"

"I don't know. A lot, probably."

"Then he's probably in a lot of places. It's what happens when you try to use magic without understanding it."

Brine bowed her head. Kaya had lied to her about everything. He'd left Cassie and the others to die on Orion's Keep when it fell. He'd tried to steal the *Onion*. But he was also the only person she remembered on this island.

"Marfak's Peak is about to explode," said Marfak West. "You might want to do something."

Brine shook her head and slid down the wall onto the floor. She felt the faint thudding of magic through her feet, a regular beat, like someone was banging a drum, and she wished it would stop.

But then the beat formed a rhythm and the rhythm took on words.

Finish this.

A thrill ran through her. She had a family, Brine thought. Her parents were only part of it. There was Cassie, and Peter and Tom, the whole crew of the *Onion*. All the people who made her the person she was. And, somewhere in the world, her parents would be looking for her. Brine knew they would, because she knew them. They would never give up until they found her, and she wasn't going to give up, either.

The floor trembled until the vibrations ran up through her, and her whole body pulsed in time with it. She'd never quite been able to work out what it was, but now she knew. It wasn't, as Peter kept saying, the magic that filled the ship. It was the sound of a heartbeat.

Brine climbed to her feet. "The *Onion* isn't just the ship. It's the crew. It's Cassie. It's the story. And stories are living things; they keep changing."

Marfak West nodded slowly.

This ship was not only the *Onion*. It had belonged to Aldebran Boswell, the scientist and explorer who had tried to find Magical North and had died there. A century sleeping in the most magical place in the whole world, a place steeped in stories and legend until eventually it had become Orion's ship—the ship that flew to the stars.

But the story of Orion was different here. Orion wasn't a ship: She was a dragon.

"I can help you," said the ghost.

Marfak West always had wanted to be the star of the story. Brine walked past him and picked up Kaya's staff. "It's all right. I know what to do."

The ghost sighed, and faded. Brine found that she didn't hate him anymore. She wondered what had changed inside her.

You can tell a story and make it come true, Kaya had said. Of course she could, because all stories had truth at their hearts. All she had to do was find it.

Echoing the ghost's sigh with one of her own, she tucked the magus's staff under her arm and climbed the ladder to the deck.

CHAPTER 34

There is no do or don't do. Trying is all that matters.
(from BRINE SEABORNE'S BOOK OF PLANS)

Peter had no magic left. There was nothing he could do to stop the falling balloon, and yet he tried to do something anyway. He ran, his arms outstretched, reaching up for Stella. As she fell, Boswell plunged down out of the sky, caught her clothes, and flapped his wings madly. She slowed then plowed straight into Peter, and both of them fell. Something in Peter's leg tore painfully. His head bounced off a stone, and bright sparks of light danced in front of his eyes. He came to a halt and lay panting, wondering why it was so hard to breathe, until he noticed Stella lying on top of him. Bits of shredded balloon drifted gently down.

Peter elbowed Stella off. "Are you alive?"

"I can hear you, so I guess so." She picked herself up, groaning. "That hurt."

Boswell landed beside them. Stella flung her arms around

the dragon. "Well done," she said. She met Peter's gaze. "What do we do now?"

Patches of grass burned all around them. The fire was spreading quickly across the dry slopes and—Peter was sure it wasn't just his imagination—the crack in the mountainside just above them gaped wider and redder. And amid the shattered rocks, something moved.

Peter got up, ignoring the pain in his leg, and hobbled back up Marfak's slope to the place where the eggs had hatched.

"Look," whispered Stella in awe.

Baby dragons.

Two were as red as the fires around them, and the other two were the color of polished bronze. They snapped angrily at Boswell as he bent to sniff them, and he drew back, looking surprised and somewhat offended.

There ought to be some ceremony for this, Peter thought, but there wasn't time. He grabbed the two red dragons and cradled them in his arms while they bit and clawed at him. One of them breathed fire at his chest, setting his shirt alight.

Stella bent to pick up the other two. One of them cowered flat and bit her, and the other one backed away fast, its bronze wings whirring. Boswell darted after it while Peter beat out the flames on his shirt one-handedly.

"We're trying to help you, you stupid animals," said Stella, making a grab for the little bronze one as it kept retreating.

Boswell pounced, trying to pin the dragon to the ground,

but it slithered out from underneath him and dashed away. Peter gasped a warning, too late. The ground split with a roar, lava spurted out, and the bronze dragon hopped back again into the bubbling mass and disappeared.

Stella stumbled back, away from the molten rock.

"It's all right," said Peter. It wasn't, but he couldn't think of what else to say. "You tried—and we have three dragons. Three out of four is good, isn't it?"

Stella wiped her eyes on her palm. The remaining bronze dragon twisted in her grip, trying to escape. "I'm sorry," she said. "I should have been faster."

"You should have been in the balloon, staying away from here."

Boswell nosed Peter's hand as if in commiseration. The baby red dragons stopped blowing fire and went back to biting and clawing. Peter turned them around so they couldn't reach him, and hobbled painfully to his feet. The smoke from the volcano must have been affecting his eyes, because tears were running down his face. "We should go higher if we can," he said. "If we can get above the eruption, we may be safe."

The ground shook as they began to walk, and more cracks opened around them. Stella pulled Peter on as he stumbled. "Can you magic us out of here?"

"Sorry," he coughed. "The eggs took all the magic when they hatched. Don't worry. We'll be fine."

"You have a strange definition of fine."

"I know. I get it from Cassie."

They stumbled on together, but as fast as they climbed, the fire seemed to follow them. *Keep together and keep hold of the dragons*, Peter thought. Nothing else mattered. Although he would like it if the little creatures would stop attacking him for one minute. He clutched them tight against his chest with one arm and clung on to Stella with his free hand. Boswell flapped ahead, circling back and shooting little flames at them to urge them on faster.

Below, the mountain was falling apart. Rocks crashed down, some of them splintering into pieces that kept tumbling on until the splinters turned to dust. Molten lava spilled through the spaces they left, slowly at first, then turned into a sizzling black-and-scarlet flood that rolled on down toward the sea, where the waves swallowed it harmlessly, sending up huge clouds of yellow steam.

"We did it," said Stella, shouting over the noise of falling rock. "Marfak is erupting out to sea. We've saved Apcaron."

Peter nodded, gasping for breath. The ground rumbled as if there really were a dragon trapped inside the mountain. Maybe later they could celebrate, but right now his lungs were full of smoke, and he could barely see through the ash that filled the air.

He took another step and the mountain quaked. He staggered, losing his grip on the two red dragons. As he reached for them, his foot caught in a hole, his knee wrenched, and his whole leg buckled underneath him.

"Peter!" cried Stella. She crawled back to him. Boswell herded the red dragons into her arms and sniffed at Peter, whining softly.

Peter tried to get up but a new burst of agony made him dizzy, and he collapsed again.

Stella knelt next to him. "Peter, you've got to get up."

But he couldn't: He knew he couldn't. In a way, it made things easier. It meant he could stop worrying, stop trying to do this when he knew there was no way off the mountain. He'd done his best, and it had almost been good enough—that had to count for something. "You'll have to take the dragons," he said. "Keep climbing, and don't look back."

"No," said Stella. She sat stubbornly. "I'm not leaving you. You can still walk."

"No, I can't. Sorry."

Boswell butted him with his nose. Peter pushed the dragon away. "Sorry. It's not safe here. Boswell, go. Find Brine."

Boswell whimpered and hopped back a step. "Go away!" Peter shouted, hating himself. He picked up a stone to throw, but he couldn't make himself do it. He let his hand fall. He couldn't hurt Boswell, not even to save the dragon's life. "Boswell," he pleaded. "You know how to fly. Fly away."

"You're hopeless," said Stella. She took the stone off Peter and threw it. Boswell jumped back, looking more startled than hurt. The next stone Stella threw hit him, and he flew up into the air. Stella sent another stone sailing after him.

The dragon cried and made as if to land again, but Stella drew her arm back and he wheeled away, still calling out.

Stella sank back to the ground then. "You know your problem," she said shakily. "You're too soft."

"I know." Peter dragged himself across to a flat rock and sat down on it. "You should go, too," he said miserably. "I really can't walk."

"I know. And I'm really not going to leave you, so don't bother arguing. I'm glad Boswell's gotten away, but I'm fine here." She settled herself comfortably on the ground beside him as if to prove the point. The baby dragons squirmed in her lap, attacking alternately her and one another.

Selfishly, Peter was glad. Even though it wouldn't make any difference if she stayed. All it meant was that she'd die along with him—the baby dragons, too.

Peter struggled to upright himself. "Seriously, you have to go," he said. "The dragons are important."

Stella lifted the bronze dragon up and stared into its face. "I didn't do this for dragons," she said at last. "I did it for Apcaron." She smiled. "That, and to stop you from getting yourself killed."

"Brine says that trying is all that matters," said Peter.

"She may be right."

They both gazed down the mountainside at the clouds of smoke and patches of boiling rock.

"I don't think I'd make it much farther anyway," said Stella. "The whole mountain is falling apart. You never know: Maybe Cassie will come to rescue us."

Yes, maybe she'd sail the *Onion* straight up the mountain to them and they'd all sail off into the sunset. That would be good. Peter reached his hand out. Without looking at him, Stella took it and closed her fingers around his.

"Nobody will know," said Peter. "Nobody will tell stories or sing songs about how brave we were."

Stella squeezed his hand. "Yes, they will. They'll tell new stories about how the dragons came back just for a little while, and the biggest and bravest dragons of all were called Peter and Stella. Peter for the earth and Stella for the stars."

And Brine for the sea, Peter thought. Brine should be in the stories somewhere—Tom, too. A flutter of movement caught his gaze—probably just a handful of burning grass, but he sat forward to look.

Something bit his hand. Peter yelped in pain, then yelped again in astonishment. A tiny bronze dragon shook itself and sneezed. Its tail was black with soot and smoke coiled from its ears.

Stella looked at the three dragons in her lap. "What?"

"It survived!" said Peter. "It must have followed us." He scooped up the dragon and dropped it again as it burned his hands.

Stella poked the dragon carefully. "It's hot. The lava should have burned it up, but it didn't even hurt it."

Different eggs, different dragons. They'd found Boswell's egg covered in ice; these dragons obviously preferred fire. Peter started to laugh, and once he'd started, he couldn't stop. He laughed until his stomach ached and tears ran down his face. "The dragons can survive in lava. We did it! They're all going to live."

CHAPTER 35

RECIPE FOR A STORY

Take a good-sized pinch of truth, one handful of adventure, and another of the best thing you can imagine. Season it well with humor, stir with goodwill, and add in as much of your own heart as you can spare. Leave to mature, taking it out every so often to test it until it's ready.

Best served shared.

(from COOKING UP A STORME—
THE RECIPES OF A GOURMET PIRATE)

Ebeko and Hiri turned in surprise when Brine walked back onto the *Onion*'s deck.

"Where's Kaya?" asked Ebeko.

Brine tried not to think about it. "He's . . . around somewhere." Her mind was a whirlwind. The two magi must have known Kaya wasn't really her father. They'd probably known her real parents, probably stood and watched while they fled the island with her and ended up who knew where. Whatever influence Kaya had had over them, one of them could have said something.

She squared her shoulders and did her best to look authoritative. "You both heard him say I was assistant captain. He's not here now, so that puts me in charge. Let the crew go, and I'll talk to them."

They were so used to taking orders that they almost obeyed her. Ebeko hesitated a few seconds, then shook her head and brushed past Brine to the hatch, Hiri following. Brine stayed where she was. She could feel the ship's heartbeat through her feet, so loud that she was surprised the whole crew couldn't hear it.

Trudi let out a yell and flailed about.

"Danger ahoy!" shouted Tim Burre from the mast.

Rob and Bill leaped up and drew their swords.

"Everyone, calm down," said Brine. "We don't have much time, and I need you to listen." Her heart beat in time with the ship's. She let Kaya's staff go; she didn't need it. "This ship is called the *Onion* because someone once couldn't spell *Orion*," she said. "But it's more than that—much more." She took a deep breath. All around her the crew stood, confused but listening.

"When the world was young," said Brine, "the island of Apcaron was called Dragon Island because dragons came there to nest in the golden sand every spring. And the two mightiest dragons were Marfak and his sister, Orion."

The story became more real with every word. How could Brine have ever thought Orion was a sailor? Of course Orion was a dragon; she couldn't be anything else. The thrumming in the ship's boards grew louder. Less like a heartbeat now and more like the beating of wings. Out of the corner of her eye, Brine saw Ebeko come back onto the deck and stop.

Ebeko had loved Kaya, Brine thought. Maybe she hadn't seen past the facade of a man who was only ever trying to do the right thing. Or maybe she'd seen deeper still, seen through all his lies and weakness and glimpsed something underneath that was worth loving after all. When she told his story, Brine would leave some details out. Kaya had tried to save the island, too. He would be like the man trying to steer his ship between a sea-monster and a whirlpool, destruction on either side.

But first, the story of Orion needed to be told. "Year after year, the dragons fought," she said. "Sometimes Marfak would win and sometimes Orion. But at last Orion cast her brother down into the earth and sprang away, into the stars, and Marfak became a great volcano, full of fire."

"Um, Brine," said Trudi. "Something is happening to the ship. Something strange."

The *Onion* moved, as if lifted on a swell of water, but the sea was completely flat. And the world shifted and then split in two. In one half, Brine was sitting on a ship, telling a story to the enraptured crew. And in the other, she was clinging to the back of a dragon, rising out of the waves with the roar of the wind blotting out all the shouts of the crew.

She was Brine Seaborne of the *Onion*, and she was Oshima of Orion's Keep. She had ties to the island that would never break, and yet she loved the *Onion* with all her heart. She turned to face the two magi. "One day Orion will come back, and Marfak will rise out of the ground to meet her in flames," she said. "Or maybe it will be the other way around. Marfak will rise first, and then Orion will return to see his end." She laughed at the panic on Ebeko's face. "You might want to grab hold of something, by the way. This ride is going to get bumpy."

And with that, the *Onion* lifted out of the sea altogether, and the great dragon Orion spread her wings and soared into the sky. The deck changed beneath Brine's feet, one second becoming a huge scaly back, and the next shifting back to weather-beaten timber. Brine fell flat and hung on. The crew instinctively grabbed for anything that looked solid.

A second set of wingbeats cut through the sky, and Boswell came flying down. The little dragon was covered in soot and flew awkwardly as if one wing wasn't quite working. But instead of landing, he circled the deck then darted away, in the direction of the smoking mountain. Orion turned to follow, cutting through the sky like lightning.

Smoke poured from Marfak's stricken sides, and then red lava came tumbling down into the sea, where it turned the waves into boiling mist. And, high above them, the solid shape that was Orion's Keep finally wavered and began to fall.

CHAPTER 36

They tell many tales about the *Onion*. The greatest pirate ship
on the eight oceans. The only ship to have sailed to the top of
the world and returned. Now they're going to have to add
another story to that list, but I don't think anyone will believe it ever.

(from THOMAS GIRLING'S BOOK OF PIRATING ADVENTURE)

O rion's Keep tilted. The third turret slid away and tumbled
down. Tom scrabbled back from the edge, leaving the
useless length of rope and knotted sheets that were nowhere
near long enough anyway. They needed magic or another
balloon, and unfortunately neither of those were going to turn
up now.

Cassie tossed the makeshift rope over the castle wall and
started to tie the end to the battlements. "We have to do this
now. If we wait until the whole castle is falling around us, we
won't stand a chance. Tom, come on."

A writer should always be open to new experiences, Tom
thought, pushing himself unsteadily to his feet. It was how

you learned about the world, and how you learned about yourself. Besides, there was a very small chance they'd survive if they climbed down and no chance at all if they stayed where they were. Any-sized chance was better than none.

"Take it steady," said Cassie, "and don't look down. I'll be right below you. Try not to worry it could be . . ."

The stones parted by her feet. Tom yelled and grabbed hold of her, and Cassie threw him back, sending him staggering away from the castle's edge.

"Cassie!" shouted Ewan.

Tom turned, panic blotting out everything else. Cassie had disappeared. For a second Tom was certain she'd fallen and he couldn't bear to look, but then he saw her hands clinging on to the crumbling castle edge and he heard her voice. "Can someone pull me up? Quickly, if you don't mind."

Tom felt dizzy with relief.

"Stay there," commanded Ewan. Tom wasn't sure whether he was talking to him or Cassie. Both, probably. He knelt down—it felt safer that way—and started to crawl to the edge of the castle. Ewan didn't bother with crawling; he just threw himself flat, slid, and grabbed Cassie's wrists. "Hold on!"

"The thought had occurred to me."

More stones fell away. Ewan began to haul Cassie up, but then a piece of battlement right next to him broke away and he started to slide again. He wedged his feet into the broken floor and hung on, his arms straining. "I've got you," he said. "Don't worry. I won't let you go."

Tom edged forward as far as he dared. Looking over the edge, he could see Cassie's pale face, her hair streaming behind her.

"Tom, get back," Ewan snapped.

Tom shook his head and reached down to Cassie, sick with terror. But Ewan was already at arm's length, and Ewan's arms were much longer than Tom's. Tom leaned as far as he dared, but there was still a gap the length of his hands between him and Cassie.

He unrolled his sleeve and let it dangle over his fingers. The edge of it brushed Cassie's hand.

Almost. Just a little farther.

Cassie's hands slipped. She cried out, tried to catch hold of Ewan, and missed.

Ewan didn't even hesitate. He threw himself straight over the broken parapet after her. He caught up with Cassie in midair, and their hands reached for each other and clasped tight.

Ewan's voice drifted up to where Tom watched. "I won't let you go."

And Cassie's voice came in return. "I know."

Tom's eyes filled with tears. Then the battlements gave way completely, and he was falling, too.

▸┄┼┼╫●

L ook!" shouted Stella.

A shadow blotted out the sun. Peter forgot the pain in his leg and his blistered hands. He even forgot the smoldering ground for a moment. Now he knew how Ewan Hughes must have felt when the new *Onion* had come to the rescue in the ice floes of the frozen north. One moment they were sure they were going to die, and the next it was as if the whole world had been reborn around them.

The *Onion* sailed through the sky. Fire and smoke billowed around it and magic crackled like stray lightning, and in the next moment, the ship had become a dragon. It glided with wings outstretched, its tail whipping the smoke into billows behind it. Its scales ranged from glossy ebony to bright silver, and they kept changing color as Peter watched.

"It's Orion," said Stella. She stood, staring up with open-mouthed astonishment. "She's come back to see Marfak die."

Peter shook his head. No—this was Brine's doing. He didn't know how she was doing it, only that it had to be her.

The dragon dipped closer, and Peter saw Boswell. The little dragon flapped on ahead of the giant one, flying lop-sidedly, but definitely alive. Peter's heart surged. He struggled to his feet and stood painfully on his undamaged leg. The four baby dragons clung to his clothes, hissing angrily. They seemed to blame him for all this.

"I guess we're not going to die after all," said Peter, and tears started down his face again.

The dragons circled above them, flying lower. Orion's shape became more solid each time she flew around, though Peter still caught glimpses of the ship's hull through the multicolored scales.

"There's nowhere she can land," said Stella.

A rope thumped down by her feet. Peter grinned at the surprise on Stella's face. "I guess that solves that problem."

He had to let himself be hauled most of the way, his leg still refusing to support him. He sprawled onto what was either the deck of a flying ship or the back of a great dragon. The crew crowded around, and Brine's face appeared above him, filled with worry. Peter groped around in his shirt for a dragon and lifted it up for her to see. "Look. Here be dragons." For some reason, this seemed to be the funniest thing ever, and he laughed until he cried.

Stella flopped down flat next to him. "Are we alive?"

"I think so." Peter managed to catch his breath, and sat up. His body ached in a thousand different places, but at least he was alive to feel it. It could be worse.

"Where's Cassie?" he asked.

"Kaya left them in the castle," said Brine. "Ewan and Tom, too. We're going for them now."

Peter couldn't see Kaya anywhere. He wondered what had happened to the magus, and decided that this was not the best time to ask.

Orion wheeled around, and the whole deck reverberated with each beat of the dragon's wings. Below them, Marfak's Peak belched more and more smoke until, in a rush, the whole side of the volcano blew out into the sea and lava flowed in a bright-red flood, hissing and smoking and becoming solid rock as it touched the water.

At the same moment, Orion's Keep fell apart.

Orion lunged forward. Pieces of stone fell around them, but the dragon shrugged them off and, in the midst of the falling rubble, Peter saw three small figures. Two of them were holding hands. Orion folded her wings and tore down underneath them.

Cassie and Ewan landed on the deck with a crash. Half a second later, Tom fell on top of them. They all lay so still that Peter was terrified they were dead, but then Cassie groaned and lifted her head.

"Why is my ship flying?" she asked.

CHAPTER 37

Magic does not corrupt: It transforms. Resist the transformation, and it will gradually eat away at you. But accept it, and it will change you into something new and quite wonderful. Like Orion's Keep or the *Onion*.

(from THOMAS GIRLING'S BOOK OF PIRATING ADVENTURE)

Brine limped across the back of Orion and collapsed down next to Peter, Stella, and Tom. She felt emptied out, barely able to think straight, and they didn't look much better. In a daze, she watched Cassie giving orders and the pirates surrounding Ebeko and Hiri and tying them up. Brine didn't think the two magi would cause any more trouble. The loss of Kaya and the transformation of the ship into a dragon had shocked them both into inertia, and they didn't resist. Meanwhile, the great dragon Orion flew on across the island. Boswell flapped around in a frenzy of excitement, sometimes landing, then taking off again and turning somersaults in the air. The four newborn dragons finally gave up fighting. They curled up together in a red-and-bronze tangle and went to sleep.

Four new dragons, Brine thought. That was enough to start a family. She leaned over the edge of the deck—or the edge of the dragon's back, depending on their point of view—and watched the treetops skim along far below. When Orion passed over the coast, Brine thought she could see people waving, and she waved back.

"What's going to happen down there now?" she wondered aloud.

Stella ran her hand over the deck/scales. "Cerro and Marapi will have to sort something out. I guess the magi will join us in the village. What did happen to Kaya?"

His name sent a sharp pain through Brine's chest.

"You can tell us later," said Peter.

Brine shook her head. She'd had enough of secrets. "Kaya wasn't my father," she said. "My parents were magi in the castle. Kaya was using me to create magic, and they tried to escape with me. I ended up on the other side of the world, alone, but they may still be alive somewhere. Marfak West told me—I met his ghost."

Tom's eyes became round. "Marfak West's ghost is really here?"

"He is. Sorry I didn't believe you before, Peter." She should have trusted him more. She ran her hands over her face and sighed. "Anyway, Marfak West told me the truth, and Kaya admitted it. And then Kaya tried to take control of the ship, but he couldn't do it, and all the spells in his staff tore him apart."

Telling the story meant that she saw it happen again, flashing through her memory like fire. "I'm going to tell the islanders a different story," she said. "Kaya spent his life protecting the island, and he deserves to be remembered for that."

Nobody said anything for a while.

Tom took out the spellstone that Hiri had given him and turned it over and over in his hand. "Where are Brine's parents?" he asked.

A blade of amber light streaked out, then the last magic in the stone gave out and it turned gray.

Brine started.

Peter took the starshell. "I'll try again later. We might need more magic to find them."

Brine sat back down and hugged her arms around herself. Her parents were alive. They were still lost, but still alive.

"I can remember them now," she said. "I know what they look like. My mother was tall, even taller than my father. She used to tell me stories—about dragons."

><++}}}‹•

Orion made one more circuit of the island. The people hiding in the village came out to stand and stare. And on the beach, six children—four boys and two girls—who had been staring at the waves with blank eyes suddenly jumped up.

Cerro didn't notice at first—like everyone else, he was staring into the sky. But then he heard Ren's voice and turned awkwardly on his crutches.

Ren ran to him. "Cerro, why is there a dragon in the sky? And why are your legs funny?"

Cerro crumpled down into the sand, laughing. He saw the other five children all talking, looking around for their families. Brine had said something about dragons maintaining the balance of magic, he remembered. He didn't know what had just happened, but stories had always talked about Orion returning, and it was entirely possible that the dragon's return would put everything back the way it should be.

He watched as Orion flew out to sea, then folded her wings and sank down onto the waves. When he blinked, all he saw was a ship, small and fragile. He put his arm around Ren's shoulders. "Of course there's a dragon," he said. "This is Dragon Island."

CHAPTER 38

Today's monster warnings: Attention all merchants, fisher-
men, pirates, and other sailors. There are no further severe
monster warnings. Please be on your guard for existing monsters, but it appears that the current crisis has stabilized.

(from STRANGE TIDES: JOURNAL OF THE UNEXPLAINED AND
INEXPLICABLE, Submitted to Barnard's Reach by news-scribe)

The village gates were shut fast. Brine had half expected this. There had been no word from Marapi all night, though she must have seen Orion flying. The group of islanders, pirates, and dragons stopped outside the gates, and Cerro limped forward and banged on them. The healstones had left him weak, but he was walking without crutches again.

"Marapi!" he shouted. "I know you can hear me. You have a choice: Open these gates, or our magi will break them down."

One of the first things Cerro had done that morning was to speak with Hiri and Ebeko. Brine, waiting at the back of the group, actually felt a bit sorry for the pair. They'd spent an uncomfortable night tied up on the beach, waiting to see if the pirates would decide to throw them into the sea. But in the morning, Cerro had given them a choice: Join him and follow orders, or Peter would magic them far out to sea in one of the pirates' rowing boats. They'd chosen to stay.

The village gates opened. Marapi waited inside, wielding a spear in her hand, and behind her, at least fifty villagers stood ready and armed.

"You're not welcome here," said Marapi. "You left the village, and you are outsiders now. Go."

Cerro stared at her incredulously for a second, then he laughed. "Are you serious? Marfak's Peak erupted out to sea; Orion's Keep fell. Didn't you see the dragon flying?"

The scars on Marapi's face twisted. "Dragons exist only in stories. We saw a mirage, caused by magic and the volcano's smoke. You can't . . ."

She broke off, her mouth open, as Cassie stepped aside to reveal Stella, Peter, Brine, and Tom, each holding a small, furious dragon.

"Lizards," said Marapi. Her voice was desperate. "Some new breed of teradon, no doubt."

Boswell approached and torched her spear with flames.

"Dragons," said Cerro firmly as Marapi stamped out the fire.

Brine stifled a giggle. A few other people laughed, too: The islanders around her, but also some of the villagers standing behind Marapi. The dragon squirmed in her arms, trying to bite through the leather padding she'd wrapped around her arms. These four dragons were nothing like Boswell. When Boswell set you on fire, it was an accident; these babies did it on purpose. And they fought over food and snapped at anyone who came near them. They seemed to have accepted that Boswell was in charge, but Brine wondered how long that would last.

When she'd imagined a world with dragons, she'd pictured them all like Boswell—cute and friendly, a bit clumsy. A world with wild dragons was a very different place—bigger, and more exciting. The dinosaurs were going to be in for a shock.

Cerro walked through the village gates, and people moved back to make way for him. "Everything is changing," he said, stopping in the middle of them. "Marfak's Peak is dormant for now, but we still need magic. And we are Dragon Island, home to the only dragons in all the eight oceans."

Stella stepped close to Marapi. "You can back him up," she said quietly, "or I'll tell him about the teradons you sent to kill Peter and me."

Marapi glowered at her. "You have no proof."

"Is that what you think?" The girl raised her eyebrows, striding away.

"Do you have proof?" whispered Brine.

Stella gave her a tight-lipped smile. "No, but don't tell her that."

"Where is Kaya?" Marapi called.

Ebeko looked at the ground, biting her lip. Hiri scuffed the ground uneasily.

"He's dead," said Brine. She shut her eyes for a moment. Two things could be true in the same moment. A ship could also be a dragon, and a liar could also be a hero. She drew in a deep breath and opened her eyes again. "Kaya died trying to save Orion's Keep. He was already ill because of the strain of keeping all those spells going, and he needed so much magic at the end that it was too much for him. It's thanks to him that we're here now."

That was true enough, in a way. If it hadn't been for Kaya, Brine's parents would never have sent her across the world. She would never have met Peter, or joined the *Onion*.

Ebeko's expression softened, and she nodded at Brine before following Cerro into the village. Whether it was in thanks or warning, Brine did not know. Possibly it was both.

Brine turned away. The stories would grow just as all stories did, and in years to come, they'd turn Kaya into the hero who'd sacrificed himself so that the island and the dragons could live.

It took several hours for Cerro and Marapi to come to an agreement.

"It will be difficult for a while," said Cerro, emerging from his hut to watch Boswell trying to teach the baby dragons how to fly. "I could have thrown her out of the village, and she knows it. She's lost her power. But it's time we started working together. The dragons will be safe here."

"Thank you," said Brine. She looked around at the village, taking in the familiar circle of huts and the dragons snapping and growling as they spread their wings. She smiled.

"You could stay," offered Cerro. "We'd be glad of your help." His gaze shifted over Brine's head. "What do you say, captain?"

Brine knew what Cassie would say. This morning she'd caught her going through some of the boxes that the magi had left on the *Onion*. One of them had contained maps.

"We'll stay for a few days," said Cassie. "Just until things are settled here and we've restocked the ship." She glanced sideways, catching Brine's gaze. "Of course, if any of my crew decides to stay on, we'll talk about it."

Brine shook her head. Part of her knew she'd be sorry to leave—but she'd be even sorrier if she stayed. Even with dragons to take care of, she could never be happy staying in one place. She'd come here looking for home and family, and she'd found neither. Orion's Keep lay in pieces all over the slopes of the volcano, and her parents could be anywhere between here and the other side of the world. She couldn't give up looking for them.

"The *Onion* is where we belong," she said. "Right?"

"Right," said Tom at once.

Peter didn't answer. Brine kicked him.

"I'm still deciding," he said seriously.

Boswell crashed into the roof of a hut, but Brine barely noticed. "Peter!"

eter stepped away from her. "Brine, will you stop kicking me? There are dragons here, and the island needs magic."

"But we need you!" She couldn't have gotten through the days in Orion's Keep without him.

Peter shook his head. "Brine . . ." Then he turned and walked away.

Cassie put a hand on Brine's shoulder. "Leave him be," she murmured.

"What for? So he can decide to leave us?"

"No, so he can decide what he wants without you interfering. We all want him to stay on the *Onion*, but if you push him to do it, we'll all end up regretting it. Trust me: I know what happens when people get pushed into things."

Brine paused and watched as Peter joined Stella. The two of them started trying to round up the baby dragons. He seemed taller, Brine thought, or maybe he was just standing up straight for the first time. She nodded.

"Did you know that Marfak West's ghost is haunting the ship?" asked Brine, wiping her hands across her face.

Cassie's smile froze rigid. "No. Oddly enough, I didn't know that. Mr. Hughes, why do people never tell me things?"

"Because you're the captain," said Ewan. "You're supposed to know everything already. There's no such thing as ghosts. The last time we saw them, it was just a hallucin . . . a whatever that long word Tom used was."

"Hallucination," said Tom.

"He was not a hallucination," said Brine. "I talked to him. He helped me."

Ewan grinned. "There you are, then—definitely not Marfak West."

Brine wasn't so sure.

"We'll search the ship when we get back," said Cassie, and Brine had to be content with that.

EPILOGUE

Are you hoping to see something legendary,
A sight you can long feast your eye on?
Sail forth on a quest to the magical west
And you might see the dragon Orion.
Oh, her scales are all shades and her wings are cascades
Of such beauty they'll blow off your socks.
For one chance to spy on the dragon Orion
A man would walk barefoot on rocks.

(from THE BALLAD OF ORION)

Over the next week, Peter divided his time between the *Onion* and the island. Hiri wanted to learn how to cast spells straight from starshell, and though Ebeko muttered about the dangers of wild magic, she, too, watched as Peter demonstrated.

Meanwhile, Brine was spending hours with Boswell, and Tom read his way steadily through the books saved from the castle library. Peter was glad they all had things to keep them busy—and Cassie had probably told everyone to leave him alone, because nobody talked to him about staying or leaving. It was bad enough when he caught Brine watching him. If he stayed here, he'd miss her and Tom and the crew, but if he left with them, what would he do then? Go back to being ship's magician? There'd be no more dragons to look after. Brine still wanted to find her parents, but she could do that just as easily without him.

He returned to the *Onion* with Stella that evening to find Tom bouncing with excitement.

"What's up?" asked Peter. "Have you finally figured out why there are exceptions to the 'magic corrodes' rule?"

Tom shook his head, grinning from ear to ear. "No, this is much better. Guess what I've found."

He unrolled a sheet of paper. It was just an ordinary map—a map of the Western Ocean—but they didn't really need one of those now. Peter looked closer. "I don't see . . ."

"That's because you're not looking properly," said Tom. He pointed to where Apcaron was labeled. "See this cross? Now, look at all the others."

Peter peered at the faded writing. He counted twenty or so crosses altogether. Tom took the map off him and turned it over. On the back, someone had written: *X= nesting places.*

"Nesting places," said Tom. "We know what nested on Apcaron, don't we?"

Dragons.

Tom passed the map to Cassie, who passed it on to Ewan. The pirate groaned. "I know where this is headed. We have a crate of gold, enough supplies to take us halfway home, and we can go in any direction we please from here. We could be the richest ship on the eight oceans."

"And then what will we do?" asked Cassie. "The *Onion* is a ship with the heart of a dragon. Maybe we were even made especially just for this. To sail in search of lost islands and all the forgotten dragon eggs of the world. Think of the stories if we succeed."

Peter was already thinking. He was thinking that, knowing Cassie, she'd just sail off in some random direction and wave her sword at people, expecting dragon eggs to drop out of the sky. They needed to plan this properly, and Brine couldn't do all the planning on her own. She needed someone who knew about dragons, and she needed magic.

"We should fill some extra crates with sand," he said slowly. "We may need somewhere to store the eggs we find."

Stella's jaw dropped, but Brine flung her arms around him. "You're staying with us!"

"For now." He pushed his hands into his pockets. "I think I might come back here to live one day, but not just yet. We'll be coming back to visit, anyway, and we'll need somewhere to bring any eggs we find. This island is a good place for dragons to grow up."

"I'll look after them," said Stella.

"Or you could come with us," offered Brine. "Cassie won't

mind. You said once before that you wanted to leave the island and see the world."

Stella shook her head. "I still do, but not yet. Cerro needs me—and so do the dragons." Her gaze drifted to the sky. "I'm going to build another balloon, though. Look out for me—I'll probably come flying past you one day."

Peter held out his hand. "Good luck."

"You, too."

Peter felt the *Onion*'s heartbeat quicken. The ship was eager for the open sea and new adventures. "When can we start?" he asked.

The space beneath the deck was quiet. Tom's messenger gull slept in its cage. Zen was clearly missing Boswell and had curled up despondently in his basket. They were all going to miss Boswell, Peter thought as he made his way to the back of the ship.

The air stirred.

"You're still here, then," said Peter.

Marfak West leaned back against the crates. "Of course I'm still here. Where else would I go? Besides, I want to see what happens."

"Happens to what?"

The ghost brushed some imaginary fluff from his nonexistent sleeve. "To you, among other things. Your librarian friend has some interesting theories about magic. Magic does not corrupt; it changes. You accept the change, like the *Onion*, or resist it."

"And?" asked Peter.

"And you have had a piece of starshell in your hand for months now. What is it doing to you, do you think?"

Peter blinked, and he was alone.

ACKNOWLEDGMENTS

The island of Apcaron is an anagram of Caprona: the original *Land That Time Forgot*. This movie, and others like it, filled my childhood with stories of forgotten lands and sparked a life-long love of magical voyages and fantastical monsters. I am incredibly lucky that I can now add my own stories to the mix.

My thanks to the fabulous Julia Sooy and Rachel Kellehar, whose editing pens are mightier than many swords, and to the whole team at Henry Holt and Macmillan UK for their hard work and enthusiasm. And special thanks to Becka Moore (UK), Oriol Vidal (US), and the design teams for such stunning covers.

My agent, Gemma Cooper, who deserves a medal for her tireless hard work.

Thank you, Team Cooper; all the Sweet Sixteens; SCBWI Wales; all at St. Marks, Cardiff; my former colleagues at Cardiff University. You have provided exactly the right blend of advice, support, and friendship on this exciting journey. I'm especially grateful to Kali Wallace for reading my early draft, and Sarah Schauerte Reida, who is the best critique partner an author could hope for.

Once again, thank you to my husband, Phillip, and all my wonderful friends who have flown kites with me, played games with me, fed me brownies, and otherwise kept me more or less sane.

Finally, a gigantic, dinosaur-sized thank-you to all the wonderful booksellers who have spread the word about Brine, Peter, Tom, and the crew. Especially Seonaid in Oxford. Your support has been overwhelming and I am amazingly grateful.